Ruth's

Amish Words of Faith

THE AMISH WOMEN OF LAWRENCE COUNTY SERIES - BOOK 7

Tracy Fredrychowski

ISBN: 979-8990610590 (paperback)

ISBN: 979-8990610583 (digital)

Cover Design by Tracy Lynn Virtual, LLC

THE HOLY BIBLE, NEW INTERNATIONAL VERSION®, NIV® Copyright © 1973, 1978, 1984, 2011 by Biblica, Inc.™ Used by permission. All rights reserved worldwide.

Published in South Carolina by The Tracer Group, LLC

https://tracyfredrychowski.com

Tracy Fredrychowski

To my daughter, Laura Ann.

Like Wilma in this story, you possess a strength that inspires and a heart that radiates love. This story is a reflection of your resilience and your humor in the face of life's challenges.

By Tracy Fredrychowski

AMISH OF LAWRENCE COUNTY SERIES

Secrets of Willow Springs – Book 1

Secrets of Willow Springs – Book 2

Secrets of Willow Springs – Book 3

APPLE BLOSSOM INN SERIES

Love Blooms at the Apple Blossom Inn

An Amish Christmas at the Apple Blossom Inn

NOVELLA'S

The Amish Women of Lawrence County

An Amish Gift Worth Waiting For

The Orphans' Amish Christmas

An Amish Christmas Table: Love Beneath the Pine

THE AMISH WOMEN OF LAWRENCE COUNTY

Emma's Amish Faith Tested – Book 1

Rebecca's Amish Heart Restored – Book 2

Anna's Amish Fears Revealed – Book 3

Barbara's Amish Truth Exposed – Book 4

Allie's Amish Family Miracle – Book 5

Savannah's Amish Ties That Bind – Book 6

Ruth's Amish Words of Faith – Book 7

Katie's Amish Journey of Hope – Book 8

A WILLOW SPRINGS MYSTERY ROMANCE

The Amish Book Cellar – Book 1

The Amish Baker Caper – Book 2

The Amish Widow's Last Stitch – Book 3

www.tracyfredrychowski.com

Contents

A NOTE ABOUT AMISH VOCABULARY

The Amish language is called Pennsylvania Dutch and is usually spoken rather than written. The spelling of commonly used words varies from community to community throughout the United States and Canada. Even as I researched this book, some words' spelling changed within the same Amish community that inspired this story. In one case, spellings were debated between family members. Some of the terms may have slightly different spellings. Still, all came from my interactions with the Amish settlement near where I was raised in Northwestern Pennsylvania.

While this book was modeled upon a small community in Lawrence County, this is a work of fiction. The names and characters are products of my imagination. They do not resemble any person, living or dead, or actual events in that community.

Dear Readers,

As you step into Ruth's story, I want to share something close to my heart. Her journey mirrors my own experience with a life-changing diagnosis. Walking through the uncertainty of breast cancer was one of the hardest seasons of my life, yet it was also one of the most faith-building. By clinging to God's promises and trusting in His Word, I found strength and peace I didn't know was possible.

The main lesson I learned during this time was how powerful our words truly are. I made a conscious decision not to let negative talk or unhealthy words escape my lips, and that choice put me on a path where God showed up in ways I never imagined. The Bible reminds us that life and death are in the power of the tongue, and speaking words of faith and hope can shift our hearts and minds toward God's promises, even in life's darkest moments. It's a practice I carry with me to this day, and I hope Ruth's story reflects the strength that comes from choosing life-giving words.

Like Ruth, I learned that challenges can deepen our trust in God and open doors to share His love with others. It's often in the midst of life's hardest moments that we discover our greatest purpose. I pray that as you read Ruth's story, you'll see how God's grace can shine brightly, even in the darkest valleys. He walks with us, and His presence brings hope and healing in ways only He can.

This story is a reflection of my testimony—a testament to the power of prayer, the beauty of community, and the unshakable faith that grows when we keep our eyes fixed on Him. It's also a reminder that God uses our struggles to encourage others, showing His goodness through the stories we share.

Thank you for allowing Ruth's journey to touch your heart. My prayer is that it brings you hope, encouragement, and a deeper sense of God's unfailing love.

With love and blessings,

Tracy

LIST OF CHARACTERS

Ruth Yoder. A nurturing Amish woman who becomes like a mother figure to Wilma.

Levi Yoder. Ruth's steadfast and loving husband.

Wilma Nettles. A young English woman fighting cancer and rediscovering her faith.

Seth Trenton. Wilma's devoted boyfriend, offering unwavering support.

Janel Michales. Wilma's loyal best friend from college.

MAP OF WILLOW SPRINGS

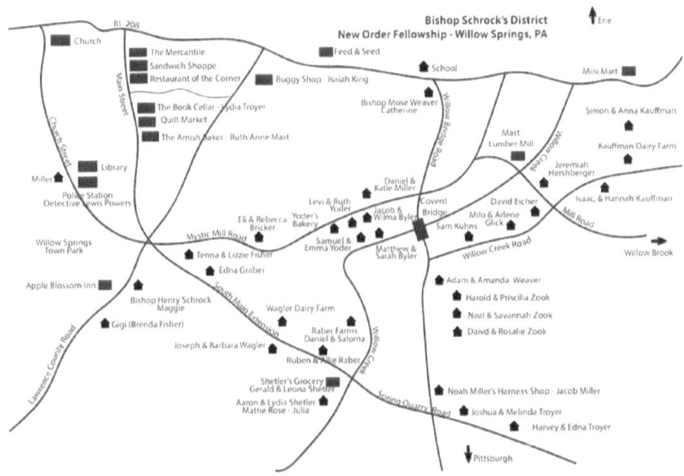

Tracy Fredrychowski

PROLOGUE
Willow Springs, Pennsylvania

I'll never forget the chill of that sterile room as I sat waiting for the doctor to read my scans. The low murmur of the technicians made me uneasy, especially when they retook images with painstaking care. A thousand thoughts tumbled through my mind, but none weighed heavier than the idea that my grandchildren might grow up without their *grossmommi* guiding them into adulthood.

And then there was Levi. How would he fare without me? His strong, steady presence just beyond those closed doors was the only thing that kept me from breaking down in tears right then and there. That, and the knowledge that showing emotion in a public place full of strangers would reveal a vulnerability I wasn't ready to expose.

After I completed the tests, the nurse kindly but firmly directed me back to the waiting room to await the doctor's call.

Each step felt heavy, like I was walking toward something that could shatter the life I knew. And yet, all I could think about was finding Levi, comforting myself in his arms' warmth, as if his touch could make sense of the senseless.

I had just celebrated my sixtieth birthday. Shouldn't I be enjoying the fruits of a long, full life? Instead, I was facing a diagnosis that might change everything... for me, for my family, for Levi. My heart was heavy with thoughts of what might come, but when I pushed through the double doors and saw him waiting for me, my world stilled for just a moment.

Levi offered a small, quiet smile when I sat beside him. We didn't need to speak. The silence between us was sacred, and his presence was a balm for the fear I was desperately trying to contain. Around us, the waiting room was filled with people in various stages of illness, some fragile and thin, others more vibrant, their laughter surprising in such a place. I wanted to be anywhere but here. The air seemed thick with the weight of what we all dreaded.

And yet, I couldn't help but feel ashamed of my thoughts. I had always leaned on my faith, trusted that *Gott* would guide us through even the darkest moments. But here I was, struggling against the tide of my own fear, trying to cling to the things I could control.

We were out of place here... *Englischers* gave us polite nods but mostly kept to themselves. I shivered slightly, pulling my sweater tighter. Levi noticed and shifted closer, his arm brushing against mine, offering me his warmth without a word.

Our love had never needed grand gestures, it had always been in the quiet moments, in the way we simply were together. Levi... my silent protector. The man *Gott* had chosen for me, and the one I couldn't imagine living without.

The weight of the room pressed down on me, and I closed my eyes, seeking some small refuge in my memories. My mind conjured an image of my best friend, Stella Byler. She had passed many years ago, but in moments like this, I longed for her presence. I could almost hear her voice, calm and reassuring, telling me that everything would be alright.

How I wished I could talk to her now, lean on her wisdom, her love. But instead, I sat in silence, feeling the ache of her absence, my fears like a weight on my chest. Levi's hand found mine for only a second, his strong fingers wrapping around mine, giving a gentle squeeze. No words were needed. It was a promise... a quiet vow that whatever came, we would face it together.

Tears welled in my eyes, but I blinked them back. I had to be strong... for Levi, our children, and our grandchildren. The road ahead was unknown, but I knew one thing: With faith, love, and my family by my side, I would face whatever lay ahead.

As the minutes dragged on, the waiting gnawed at me, every second pulling me deeper into my own thoughts. I whispered a prayer, barely audible, asking for strength, for courage, for grace. Levi took a deep breath beside me, and when I looked at him, I saw the same fear I felt reflected in his eyes. But there was something else too... unwavering love and determination. In that moment, I knew we would lean on the only strength that had ever carried us... *Gott's.*

CHAPTER 1

As Ruth sat waiting for her name to be called, her attention drifted to a young *Englischer* woman seated across from her and Levi. The worry on the young woman's face was unmistakable as she sat alone, staring out the window.

Beyond the glass, the courtyard was full of life, with bright yellow daffodils stretching toward the sun, and delicate crocuses in shades of purple and white blooming all around. On any other day, the warmth of the sun and the sight of spring bursting into color would have brought Ruth peace. But at that moment, her heart was drawn to the young woman, whose silent suffering was all too apparent.

When the young woman's gaze finally shifted and their eyes met, Ruth offered a gentle smile. "The sun is beautiful today, *jah*?"

The woman rubbed her arms, shivering slightly. "I don't understand why they keep it so cold in here."

Ruth pulled her sweater tighter around her shoulders and nodded. "I imagine it's their way of keeping the air fresh, to ward off germs. But it doesn't make the waiting any more comfortable, does it?"

The woman shrugged; her voice quiet. "No."

Something about her vulnerability tugged at Ruth's heart. She looked around the room, her thoughts momentarily drifting to the weight of her own uncertainty. But then her gaze returned to the young woman. Ruth sensed that she wasn't just battling the cold but the overwhelming fear that comes with facing the unknown.

"Is this your first time here?" Ruth asked.

The woman nodded, "Yes."

Ruth felt an urge to ease the young woman's discomfort. She knew all too well how heavy the waiting could feel, especially without a familiar hand to hold. "It's my first time too," she offered, her tone reassuring. "It's not easy, is it? I mean the waiting and all."

The young woman glanced up at Ruth, and the tension in her brow eased for a moment. "No, it's not."

A silence settled between them, but it wasn't the kind that felt awkward or heavy. Instead, it was a shared quiet, an understanding that neither had to explain aloud. Ruth could see the fear in the woman's eyes, a reflection of the same emotions Ruth had been struggling with since she'd stepped through the clinic doors. But she also knew that a small act of kindness could bring light into a dark moment.

"I'm Ruth Yoder," she said, her voice calm and kind.

"Wilma Nettles," the young woman replied, her voice still soft but a little steadier now.

Ruth nodded, sensing the girl's discomfort, but also the faintest hint of relief that someone had reached out to her.

After a moment, Wilma's hands trembled slightly as she clasped them in her lap. "I... I wasn't expecting this," she said, her words were a mere breath of a sound. "I just came in for my yearly checkup."

Ruth's heart went out to her. She understood that feeling, the weight of facing something terrifying without knowing what lay ahead. Ruth leaned forward just enough to show Wilma her sincerity. "We're both here, walking a similar path, *jah*?"

Wilma looked up, and though her expression was still worried, there was now a flicker of something else... perhaps hope, or at least a sense of shared understanding. "It's hard not to feel nervous," she said calmly.

Ruth nodded, knowing exactly what Wilma meant. "It is," Ruth agreed. "But we aren't meant to carry these burdens alone. Sometimes *Gott* sends us people to share the weight, even if only for a little while."

A faint smile appeared on Wilma's face for the first time, scarcely there but enough for Ruth to see. "Maybe," Wilma whispered.

The two women sat in silence, the cold air of the waiting room pressing against their skin like an unwelcome reminder of the sterile, uncertain place they found themselves in. The occasional shuffle of footsteps and the distant murmur of quiet conversations created a backdrop of sound that only deepened the stillness between them.

Yet, through the large window, the sun streamed in, its warmth a gentle contrast to the chill that had settled into their bones, offering a small comfort in an otherwise clinical space.

In that shared silence, they both felt it... a quiet connection, as if the sunlight itself was binding them together, two strangers who, without a word, had become silent allies in a battle neither had expected to fight.

The stillness between them was interrupted by the soft creak of the adjoining door opening. Ruth's heart quickened as she heard her name called, the nurse's voice polite but steady, as though it carried the gravity of what lay ahead. The sound pulled her from the quiet connection she had found with Wilma, snapping her back into the harsh reality she was about to face.

Levi stirred beside her, his hand instinctively reaching for hers as they rose to their feet. The warmth of his grip grounded her, but it did little to quell the flutter of anxiety that had taken root in her chest. She turned to Wilma, who met her gaze with wide, understanding eyes... no words needed to pass between them. Wilma's presence had been a reminder that even in the deepest moments of fear, *Gott* often sent comfort, whether through a familiar hand or a stranger's silent companionship.

Ruth gave Wilma a slight nod, offering a reassuring smile before stepping away. With Levi's steady presence at her side, she walked toward the door, each step feeling heavier than the last.

The nurse led them down the hall, the muted step of her shoes on the tiled floor creating a rhythmic pulse in Ruth's ears, louder than the rising beat of her own heart. Levi placed a reassuring hand on the small of her back, and she breathed in deeply, trying to steady herself, to lean on the quiet faith that had always carried her through. She whispered a prayer under her breath, a silent plea for strength and grace for whatever news awaited her beyond the door.

Together, she and Levi stepped inside, the door clicking softly shut behind them, sealing them in the moment they had both dreaded and anticipated. Ruth braced herself, knowing that the next words spoken in this room would change the course of their lives... yet trusting, as always, that whatever was to come, they would face it with *Gott's* guidance and love.

***

The cold air bit Ruth's cheeks as she waited for Levi to prepare the buggy for the long ride home. The sun shone brightly overhead, a deceptive contrast to the chill that settled in the air and in Ruth's heart. The doctor's words still echoed in her mind, heavy and unrelenting, as she pulled the thick quilt Levi had carefully packed up around her legs, seeking comfort in its warmth.

Levi finished securing the buggy, then climbed up next to her, the leather reins in his hand. Before setting them in motion, he reached over and squeezed Ruth's hand... a simple gesture, one of reassurance. They sat in silence for the first stretch of the journey, the rhythmic sound of the horse's hooves against the pavement filling the quiet between them.

Ruth watched the landscape pass by; familiar fields and winding roads that usually brought her peace now felt distant, as though the world had shifted beneath her. Twenty minutes had passed when Ruth broke the silence.

"I'd like to stop by Samuel and Katie's on the way home," she said, her eyes focused on the horizon ahead. "We should have the children join us for supper. It's best we tell them all at once. No sense waiting."

Levi glanced over at her; his brow furrowed in thought. "You wouldn't like to sleep on it first? It's been a long day, and I don't want you to tire yourself out with company. You've had a lot to process."

Ruth's hand moved to rest lightly on Levi's knee. "*Nee*, I'd rather speak to them sooner rather than later. Waiting will only make it harder, and its weight will be worse if we let it linger. It's important to be honest with them now, so they have time to understand."

Levi hesitated, the lines on his face deepening as he considered her words. "*Jah*, I suppose," he said slowly. "But only if you feel you're truly ready for it. You don't need to rush."

Ruth couldn't help but let out a soft laugh, her voice carrying a lightness that seemed at odds with the seriousness of their situation. "Now don't you go and baby me. I'm no invalid, and this is just a diagnosis... one we need to share with our family. They'll need time to come to terms with it, and so will we."

Levi chuckled evenly, but there was a tension in his eyes, a quiet worry he couldn't quite mask. "I just don't want to see you worn out. You've always been the strong one, but it's okay to let me shoulder some of it."

Ruth met his gaze. "And you will, *lieb*. But this is something we need to face head-on, and I want our children to know that I'm not afraid. I need you to trust that I'm capable of deciding how we handle this."

Levi nodded, his grip on the reins tightening somewhat as he guided the horse around a bend. "I just... I don't want to see you overwhelmed."

Ruth gave his knee a reassuring pat again. "We're in this together, and *Gott* is guiding us, *jah*? Our children are grown. They're strong too. We'll all find the strength we need, with faith and each other."

Levi glanced at her and gave a small nod. "You're right."

As they rode on, the cold wind whipped through the buggy, but the warmth of Ruth's quiet determination and Levi's unspoken support wrapped around them both.

***

The Yoder kitchen hummed with life as Samuel tried to keep a hold on the twins, Otto and Owen, while balancing little Cindy in his arms. The boys had already made their escape into the front room, leaving Samuel to sigh in exasperation as he turned to hang up the coats.

Katie and Daniel had arrived earlier, and their two daughters, Ella and Mary, settled calmly with a book from the chest Ruth kept for the grandchildren. The room was filled with the familiar sounds of family, the laughter, the patter of little feet, the clatter of dishes, and Ruth found herself smiling, even as her heart carried the weight of her unspoken news.

Just then, Emma bustled back into the house, her breath a little short from the quick dash outside. "Forgot the diaper case," she said with a sheepish grin, holding up the bag before setting it down near the kitchen table. "These little ones come with more things than I ever imagined!"

Ruth chuckled faintly. "*Jah*, I remember those days well."

The house was full to the brim now, and as Ruth took in the sight of her children and grandchildren bustling about, she felt the usual warmth in her heart that always came with family gatherings. But beneath that warmth, the doctor's words lingered, a quiet shadow that Ruth knew she would soon need to address. For now, though, she wanted to hold onto this moment... the lively energy, the joy of having them all under one roof.

Levi moved quietly to Ruth's side, his hand resting on her shoulder. He leaned in, his voice low so that only she could hear. "When do you want to tell them?"

Ruth glanced around the room, her eyes lingering on the little ones chasing after each other with bursts of laughter. She smiled, grateful for their presence, even as her heart ached with the weight of what was to come. "After dinner," she whispered back. "When their bellies are full, and their energy isn't so bountiful. It'll be easier once things have settled a bit."

Levi nodded, his hand giving her shoulder a comforting squeeze.

Ruth took a deep breath and carefully removed the meatloaf from the oven while Emma busied herself setting the table, working around the men and Katie, who had already settled in at the polished oak table.

It didn't take Levi long to pull Samuel and Daniel into a conversation about the upcoming strawberry season. *Yoder's Strawberry Acres* had been a cherished family tradition for years, and each spring, preparations started early, ensuring everything was in place for a successful harvest. The three men always worked closely together, eager to make each season better than the last.

"We're getting close to time for preparing the soil," Levi began. "I've already started clearing the old mulch from the beds and turning the soil. We'll need to add compost soon to enrich it before we plant."

Samuel nodded, thoughtful. "How's the soil looking this year? We had a lot of rain last fall. Are we going to need to test it again, or do you think it's holding up fine?"

"I've tested a few spots," Levi replied, tugging his long graying beard. "The pH is a little low in some areas, so we'll have to add some lime to balance it out before the new plants go in. I'll need to order more straw for mulching too. Keeps the weeds down and holds in the moisture."

Daniel chimed in. "And what about the new plants? Did you settle on the variety for this season?"

Levi nodded. "I'm thinking of going with the Seascape variety again. They did well for us last year, and they produce consistently throughout the season. I've put in an order already, and they should be here by the end of next week."

Samuel nodded. "We should get those covers out and inspect them soon, make sure they're not damaged from last season. We can't afford to lose any of the early blossoms."

"And don't forget about the fencing," Daniel reminded them. "Last year, the deer got into the lower field. We'll have to reinforce the wire and maybe put up a few more stakes."

Levi agreed. "We'll get that done before planting too. With the soil prepared, the new plants in, and the irrigation working, we should be in good shape. If the weather cooperates, we'll have another strong season."

The men exchanged nods of agreement, the familiar rhythm of farm life flowing between them.

The friendly chitchat and gentle hum of conversation

warmed Ruth's heart as she watched her family, gathered around the table, laughing and sharing stories. The coos and cries of her five grandchildren, soon to be six, filled the air, and Ruth felt a familiar lump rise in her throat. The weight of what she carried was too heavy to ignore, and she silently excused herself from the table.

In the quiet of the bathroom, Ruth closed the door softly behind her and leaned against it for a moment, closing her eyes as she tried to steady her breathing. With trembling hands, she pulled the crumpled piece of paper from her pocket, unfolding it carefully. The words stared back at her, cold and clinical... *focal invasive ductal carcinoma.* The pathology findings were malignant. Ruth swallowed hard. Even now, it was difficult to bring herself to say the word aloud. Cancer.

Levi had hardly left her side all day, his silent presence steady and comforting. But this moment... this brief, solitary moment... was hers. She needed it, if only to gather her strength before she faced her family.

Ruth knelt on the cold bathroom floor, folding her hands in her lap. With her head bowed, she whispered a small, desperate prayer.

"You are my God. You are with me. I will trust You in all

things. ”

The familiar words brought a flicker of peace, a gentle reminder of the strength she'd always drawn from her faith. She lingered there for a few moments, letting the silence fill her, before she rose and washed her face.

As she stepped back into the warm light of the kitchen, Emma and Katie had already started clearing the table. She cleared her throat, her voice catching a tad as she spoke. "As soon as we finish tidying up and the *kinner* are settled, your father and I need to talk with you all."

Katie paused, her hands still submerged in the soapy water, and turned to look at her mother, concern instantly flickering across her face. Ruth could sense the crack in her voice had sent a ripple of unease through her children.

"*Mamm*? Is something wrong?" Katie asked, her brow furrowed with worry.

Ruth offered a small smile, though she knew it was forced. "We'll discuss everything in a few minutes, she added. "Let's finish up here first."

She moved toward the sink. "Katie, you sit," Ruth insisted, pointing toward a chair. "I see weariness etched across your forehead. Let me handle the dishes."

Katie hesitated but eventually relented, patting her protruding belly as she sank into the chair. The room quieted, the earlier laughter and lightness replaced with a subtle tension.

Ruth could feel the weight of their curiosity, their concern, but for now, she focused on the task at hand, washing each dish with slow, deliberate movements. With each dish, she whispered another silent prayer. Soon, they would gather, and soon, the truth would be revealed. But for now, in these final moments of stillness, Ruth held tightly to the comfort of routine and the love that filled her kitchen, preparing herself for the difficult conversation that lay ahead.

Tracy Fredrychowski

CHAPTER 2

Wilma Nettles sat in her car in the employee parking lot of W.S. Middle School, staring out the windshield, her mind swirling with thoughts she couldn't seem to shake. She had never imagined she'd reach a point where the daily stress of dealing with middle schoolers would make her doubt her career choices.

Teaching had always been her calling, and she had postponed so much in pursuit of her goals. Settling down hadn't been a priority, not until she had her master's degree and a steady job. And certainly not until Seth Trenton's boyish charm became impossible to resist.

Seth, with his easy smile and steady presence, had been patient with her. His home remodeling business had taken off in the past year, and it was a comfort to Wilma that both of them were too busy to dwell too much on the idea of commitment.

Lately, however, she sensed something different in him... a

quiet but persistent desire to move forward and settle into the life they had tiptoed around for years.

He had started asking her questions, strange but sweet questions about her thoughts on marriage, what kind of house she dreamed of, even where she'd like to live long-term. She suspected he was scoping out fixer-uppers in the area, eager to prove that he could provide them with a wonderful home. And while part of her heart swelled at the idea, the other part... the part haunted by her doctor's warnings and the uncertainty of her health... held her back.

The third lunch bell rang, and Wilma sighed, glancing at her phone. Seth had texted her earlier about dinner, a standing invitation she had considered canceling more than once today.

She knew she should be excited. Seth was always thoughtful, always planning something that would make her smile... but her heart felt heavy. With the doctor's voice still echoing in her mind, warning her not to postpone the biopsy any longer, a feeling of dread lingered, clouding her thoughts. She had found the lump three months ago, and now it had grown. The concern in her doctor's eyes had been unmistakable during their last visit.

She tucked her phone into her purse, trying to shake off the weight of it all, but the nagging sense of doom gnawed at her. Wilma closed her eyes for a moment, remembering a few days earlier in the clinic when she had crossed paths with Ruth, the quiet, assured Amish woman who had shared the waiting room with her. The woman had exuded a sense of peace that Wilma envied. A faith, a calmness in the face of the unknown. It was something Wilma had longed for ever since her mother passed away when she was just a teenager.

Her mother's absence left a gaping hole, one that her elderly father, now in assisted living, had tried his best to fill. But it hadn't been the same. And now, facing a health challenge on her own, she felt more alone than ever.

Wilma caught her reflection in the rearview mirror and sighed. She brushed through her long, auburn hair, adding a quick coat of lip gloss as if the small action could restore some sense of normalcy. In the end, she decided she was hungry after all. Perhaps she needed the distraction. Seth was always a welcome comfort, maybe dinner with him would help clear her head. She didn't have the heart to cancel on him, not today.

With a deep breath, Wilma stepped out of the car and followed the distant rumble of fourteen-year-olds back toward her classroom. Tomorrow could wait. For now, she'd get through the day and try to find the words to tell Seth about her doctor's visit later.

***

Wilma scanned the parking lot, searching for Seth's work truck as she pulled into the lot behind *The Restaurant on the Corner* in downtown Willow Springs. The sun was dipping low in the sky, shadows dancing between the century-old buildings.

In a place dominated by the Old Order Amish community, it wasn't surprising when she had to pause for a brown-capped buggy to pass before maneuvering her car into a tight parking space. As she watched the couple in the buggy, her thoughts again drifted back to the Amish woman she had met at the clinic.

Her phone buzzed, a quick text from Seth telling her he was running late and asking her to grab a table. A small reprieve from the storm in her mind. Wilma sighed, her thoughts swirling, and made her way inside the restaurant, securing a small table by the window. It was usually her favorite spot, offering a view of the bustling street outside, but tonight, she felt disconnected from everything.

Fifteen minutes later, Seth stepped into the restaurant, his presence commanding as always. His tall, muscular frame, olive-toned skin, and neatly trimmed dark beard made him stand out in any crowd, and Wilma felt a familiar flutter in her chest as he approached. His smile was bright and effortless, the kind that always made her feel safe, like nothing bad could ever happen when he was around.

He held up a finger, signaling he'd be with her in a moment, and gave her a quick peck on the forehead as he settled into the seat across from her, his phone still pressed to his ear. He was in the middle of a call with a client, his voice warm and professional, but Wilma couldn't focus on his words. Her phone vibrated on the table before her, and her heart sank when she saw the name flash across the screen: *Dr. Jameston.*

Her stomach twisted. The call she'd been dreading. She pointed to her phone, excusing herself with a small, tense smile as she slid out of the booth and stepped outside into the cool evening air. The soft hum of traffic and the faint smell of her beloved farming community filled the streets as she answered the call, her voice trembling slightly. "Wilma speaking."

"Wilma, this is Nurse Walker, a breast navigator from Dr. Jameston's office. We received your pathology report, and I'd like to discuss it with you if this is a good time."

Wilma's legs felt weak, and she spotted a small bench just outside the restaurant's door. She sank onto it, her heart pounding as the nurse's voice continued, explaining the findings from her biopsy. The words blurred together... clinical terms she didn't fully understand... but one word stood out, sharp and clear, as if it had been written in bold across the evening sky: *cancer*.

Her breath caught. How could this be happening? She was only thirty-three. Healthy. Active. In the prime of her life. She was just beginning to settle into her career, imagining a future that stretched out ahead of her, full of possibilities. But now, it felt like the ground had shifted beneath her feet.

"Miss Nettles? Are you still there?" the woman's voice pulled her from the fog. "Do you have any questions?"

Wilma swallowed hard, trying to make sense of it all. A malignant tumor. Cancer that had spread into the surrounding breast tissue. Mastectomy. Chemotherapy. The words swirled in her mind, each one landing like a blow. She wasn't sure if she could absorb any more. "Uhm... yes, ma'am, I'm here. I'm just... trying to understand everything you're saying. It's a lot to take in all at once."

The nurse's voice softened. "I know it's overwhelming. Is there anyone with you? I can review everything again if you need more time to process."

Wilma's mind raced. Seth was just inside the restaurant, still on the phone, oblivious to the life-altering call she had just received. Should she tell him? Should she pull him into this storm that was suddenly consuming her?

"No," Wilma replied softly. "I'm... I'm alone." She paused, forcing herself to focus on her words. "But I think I understand what you're saying. So what's next?"

"I've set up an appointment with a breast surgeon for next week," she explained. "He'll be able to answer any specific questions you have and go over treatment options. In the meantime, please don't hesitate to call me if you need anything. I'm here to help you navigate this."

Wilma tried to remember the date and time of the appointment. After the call ended, she sat on the bench, typing the date and time of the appointment into her phone. The world around her continued as if nothing had changed. People walked past, a buggy drove by, and the lights from the restaurant glowed warmly onto the evening sidewalk. But for Wilma, everything had changed in an instant.

She stayed on the bench for a few moments longer, feeling as if she were in a dream, like the news she had just received wasn't real. Could this really be happening? How was she going to tell Seth? Her father? Janel? The weight of it all pressed down on her, suffocating in its intensity.

Finally, after what felt like an eternity, Wilma stood and slowly made her way back inside. The restaurant was bustling with the dinner crowd, but it felt distant, almost surreal. Seth was still sitting at their table, smiling at her as she approached, his phone call now finished.

"Sorry about that," he said, his voice cheerful as he slid his phone into his pocket. "Work stuff. You know how it is."

Wilma nodded, forcing a smile, but inside, she felt like she was drowning.

He picked up the menu as Wilma slid back into the booth across from him, his brow furrowing a little as he studied her face. "Is everything okay?" he asked, his tone warm but concerned. "You seem a little off tonight."

Seth reached across the table, his hand enveloping hers in a familiar, comforting gesture. Wilma's heart twisted in her chest, guilt settling in as she looked at him.

She swallowed, trying to keep her voice steady. "It's just...

the doctor's office called. They wanted to schedule a checkup." The words felt flimsy, barely touching the edge of the real issue.

"A checkup?" Seth's eyes searched hers, his concern deepening. "Is everything alright?"

Wilma forced a smile and waved off his question like she was swatting away a pesky fly. "Oh, yeah, it's just some thrilling *lady stuff.* You know, the kind of thing that would make your eyes glaze over and probably leave you looking for the nearest exit. Definitely not dinner conversation."

Seth raised an eyebrow, but before he could probe further, Wilma leaned back in her seat, her smile stretching wider. "Trust me, you dodged a bullet. Let's just say it involves more poking and prodding than I'd care to remember and leave it at that."

Seth's expression softened with a hint of relief, though the concern didn't entirely leave his eyes. He opened his mouth to ask more, but before he could speak, his phone buzzed on the table, vibrating insistently. Seth sighed, glancing at the screen, his brow furrowing once again.

"I'm sorry, sweetie," he said, whispering his apology. "I've got to take this. It's the contractor I've been trying to get ahold of all day."

Wilma nodded, the knot of tension in her chest loosening just a fraction as he excused himself from the table, stepping outside to take the call. As the door swung shut behind him, Wilma released a breath she hadn't realized she'd been holding.

The momentary reprieve gave her time to gather her swirling thoughts. How could she possibly explain all this to him? How could she even begin to put into words the terrifying uncertainty she was facing when she hardly understood it herself?

Her fingers traced the edge of the table absentmindedly as she stared out the window, watching Seth pace on the sidewalk, phone pressed to his ear. She knew she should tell him. He deserved to know. But what if she told him now and blew the whole thing out of proportion? What if the diagnosis wasn't as bad as it sounded once she met with the surgeon next week?

Wilma scoffed at herself, shaking her head slightly. *It's probably just a blip on the radar, nothing worth flipping everyone's world upside down over.* Doctors always liked to err on the side of drama. Maybe she'd go in next week and they'd tell her it was all some big misunderstanding. She could already picture it... *"Sorry, Miss Nettles, we got your results mixed up with someone else's. Oops!"* She'd laugh about it over coffee later, shake her head at how ridiculous the whole thing was.

Yeah, no point in making a big deal out of nothing, she told herself. Seth had enough on his plate with work, and she wasn't about to dump this in his lap unless it was absolutely necessary.

For now, she'd keep the details to herself, there was no need to start ringing alarm bells until she knew there was something to worry about.

Anyway, deep down, a part of her wasn't ready to face his reaction, to watch the shock and worry cloud his usually steady, calm demeanor. Telling him would make it real. For now, it was a nightmare she was living in alone. A nightmare that, somehow, she could still keep at bay by not speaking it into existence.

By the time Seth returned to the table, she had made up her mind. She would wait. She would tell him after her appointment with the surgeon, once she had more information, once she could say the words without breaking down. Maybe by then, she would have the strength to face it. To face *everything*.

"Sorry about that," Seth said, slipping back into the booth with a sheepish smile. "Business never stops, does it?"

Wilma managed another smile, though it felt brittle. "No worries," she replied, her voice carefully controlled. "I get it."

For the rest of the dinner, they spoke of lighter things... work, plans for the weekend, even a few laughs... but underneath it all, Wilma felt the weight of her secret pressing down, the truth lying unspoken between them like a shadow neither could see.

****

Wilma sat on the edge of her couch, staring at her phone, Janel Michaels' number glowing on the screen. Her thumb hovered over the call button as she chewed on her bottom lip. The urge to call her best friend was strong, but so was the hesitation.

It had only been two years since Janel lost her sister to cancer, and the pain was still fresh. The last thing Wilma wanted was to dredge up those memories. But what else could she do? She didn't have siblings, and she wasn't quite ready to tell Seth. She needed to talk to someone, and if anyone could handle her blend of nerves and bad jokes, it was Janel.

Taking a deep breath, Wilma hit the call button. The phone rang twice before Janel picked up, her voice as warm and familiar as ever.

"Wilma! What a nice way to start my Saturday. What's up,

my friend?"

Wilma smiled despite the situation. "Oh, you know, just calling to see if you want to make our annual 'Let's Panic About Life' trip a week early this year."

Janel chuckled. "You sound serious, which, for you, means something's either hilarious or really wrong. What's going on?"

Wilma hesitated for just a second, then decided to rip the Band-Aid off. "Well... I got a call from my doctor, and it seems I have a tumor. You know, the *probably fine, but maybe not* kind. Nothing to worry about. Unless, you know, it's *actually* something to worry about."

There was a brief pause on the other end of the line. Wilma winced, knowing Janel was probably processing the news. Sure enough, Janel's voice came back, calm but concerned. "Wilma... what kind of tumor? Are they saying it's... cancer?"

Wilma rolled her eyes, though the action didn't exactly match the weight in her chest. "Well, you know, that's the word they threw out there, but I think they're just being dramatic. Doctors, right? They always jump to the worst conclusions. For all we know, it could just be a wayward lump of stress from the past ten years. No big deal, right?"

"Wilma," Janel said, her tone soft but serious, "you're not

joking about this, are you?"

"Who, me?" Wilma scoffed, even though her heart was racing. "I never joke about things like this. Except, you know, when I do. But come on, Janel, you know me. I'm not about to go all doom and gloom over a phone call. Besides, I've got a surgeon appointment next week, and who knows? Maybe I'll get a souvenir. 'I went to the hospital, and all I got was this lousy tumor.'"

Janel let out a small laugh, but there was a tension in it, and Wilma could almost hear the wheels turning in her friend's mind.

"Wilma, I get that you're trying to stay upbeat, but this is serious. You know that, right? It's okay to feel scared."

"Who says I'm scared?" Wilma said, waving off the concern even though no one could see her. "I'm fine. Totally fine. I mean, what's the worst that could happen? Oh, right... cancer. But, hey, at least I've already got a great excuse to avoid the gym. Perks, right?"

Janel's voice softened, the humor fading. "Wilma... I'm so sorry. I wish I could be there with you right now."

Wilma felt a pang of guilt, knowing Janel was thinking about her sister. She swallowed hard, forcing herself to keep up the playful facade. "Oh, come on, don't get all mushy on me. You know I hate that. I've got this under control. I'll deal with the doctor, get some facts, and maybe I'll take up knitting. Isn't that what all cancer patients do?"

Janel sighed. "You don't have to joke your way through this, Wilma. You can talk to me. I'm here."

Wilma closed her eyes, her fingers gripping the phone tightly. She could feel the crack in her own armor, but she wasn't ready to let it break just yet. "I know, Janel. I do. But let's not panic until we actually know what's going on. It could be nothing, right? And if it is something... well, I'll cross that bridge when I get there. One melodramatic doctor's appointment at a time."

Janel hesitated, then said, "Okay. But I mean it, I'm here. Anytime you need me, even if you just want to make more terrible jokes."

"I'll hold you to that," Wilma said, forcing a light tone. "Get ready for some of my finest material. Cancer or not, I'm still hilarious."

After hanging up, Wilma stared at her phone for a long moment, the weight of the conversation sinking in. Janel was right, she didn't have to joke her way through this. But humor was the only thing holding her together right now, and without it, she wasn't sure how she'd handle the reality that was quickly closing in.

CHAPTER 3

Ruth poured herself a cup of herbal tea, wrapped her shawl around her shoulders, and headed out to the porch with her Aunt Catherine's letter in hand.

The unusually warm spring day was alive with the faint hint of green as the trees around their farm began to bud with the promise of summer. A light floral scent filled the air from the pink tulips she had planted around the porch, their delicate petals just beginning to open. In the yard, robins hopped about, searching for worms, while chickadees flitted back and forth from the bird feeder, scattering seeds at the edge of the porch.

Sighing contentedly, Ruth wrapped both hands around her mug, letting the warmth seep into her fingers as the steam kissed her nose. She inhaled deeply, savoring the fresh air, before setting the cup aside and unfolding her aunt's letter.

Dear Ruth,

I pray this letter finds you well. Spring has already turned to summer here in Pinecraft, and folks are preparing to return home from their winter getaways. Soon, the streets will quiet down, and things will once again be peaceful. While I enjoy seeing so many familiar faces during the winter months, I must admit I look forward to the calm even more.

After your last letter, I still can't believe you and Levi plan to come to Pinecraft. What a joyful visit it will be!

Ruth's heart tightened as she read the words. She had written to Catherine, asking if she and Levi could visit after strawberry season, but that had been before her diagnosis... before everything became so uncertain. Now, with her treatment looming, she wasn't sure she could keep that promise. The thought of disappointing Catherine tugged at her heart as she continued reading.

It will be hot when you arrive, but the ocean is beautiful in the summer. I'll be more than willing to brave the heat to give you your first taste of ocean air. You might want to warn Levi that once you set your eyes on Siesta Key, you may never want to return to Pennsylvania!

Ruth set the letter aside and picked up her tea again just as Levi crossed the yard and joined her on the porch swing. He sat close, wrapping his arm around her shoulders, his familiar presence instantly comforting.

"You look deep in thought," he said, "what's on your mind?"

Ruth sighed, her gaze drifting back to the letter. "It's Catherine. I'd almost forgotten I wrote to her about visiting after strawberry season. She's so excited."

"And?" Levi prompted kindly, sensing there was more.

Ruth hesitated, glancing down at her tea. "And I don't know if we can go anymore. Everything feels uncertain with the doctor's appointment next week. What if..." she paused, swallowing hard. "What if the plans we made can't happen?"

Levi gave her shoulders a reassuring squeeze. "Nothing's stopping us from going. We don't need to change anything until we know more. There's no reason to cancel our trip just yet."

Ruth exhaled, the tension in her shoulders easing somewhat, though her worries lingered. "I know. It's just... Catherine has been looking forward to it so much. I hate the thought of disappointing her."

Levi leaned in, pulling her closer to his side. "I understand, but there's no sense in getting worked up about it before we even meet with the surgeon. We'll know more next week, and then we can decide. *Gott's* plan will guide us, no matter what."

Ruth smiled, his words a comfort as always. "You're right," she said calmly. "I've already told myself that whatever happens, I trust *Gott* has walked this path before me. But I just wish I didn't have to disappoint her. She's so full of life, and the thought of breaking her heart..."

Levi kissed the top of her head. "You won't disappoint her."

Ruth squared her shoulders, drawing strength from her faith and from Levi's steadfastness. "I'm not afraid of what's coming, Levi. I trust *Gott's* plans, I truly do. It's just... we might not be able to visit after all."

Levi nodded, understanding the weight of her concerns. "We'll cross that bridge when we come to it. For now, let's hold on to our plans and trust that *Gott* will show us the way."

Levi patted her knee. "I best get back to work. That planter isn't getting fixed by me sitting here."

Ruth added, "I'm walking over to check on Katie and the *kinner* here in a few minutes. When I return, you'll be ready for dinner, *jah?*"

"Whatever you got in the oven is already making my stomach growl. I'll be ready for sure and certain."

***

Ruth heard the familiar sounds of her daughter's busy household long before she opened the door. The hum of activity, children's laughter, and the occasional cry of frustration blended into a lively commotion. When Ruth stepped inside, Katie's face softened with relief at the sight of her.

"*Mamm*," Katie breathed, her voice laced with gratitude. Without a word, Ruth moved to scoop up little Ella, who was fussing in her highchair, tears streaming down her chubby cheeks. Katie was already halfway through braiding Mary's hair, hairpins tucked between her lips, and a sheen of sweat resting on her upper lip. Ruth wiped Ella's face delicately, then gathered a few toys from the nearby basket and placed the little girl on the floor at her sister's feet.

Katie finished the last braid and sighed, leaning back in her chair. "You couldn't have come at a better moment. *Denki, Mamm.*"

Ruth smiled warmly as she brushed a loose strand of hair from Katie's face. "*Ach*, what are mothers for?" she teased gracefully before her tone turned more concerned. "Any more pains today?"

Katie shook her head, resting her hand on her belly. "*Nee,* they seem to have stopped, just like the midwife said. I think this one is staying put for a bit longer."

"*Goot*. It's a bit too early yet," Ruth said, her voice tinged with relief.

Katie glanced at her mother, her brow furrowing as she reached over to squeeze Ruth's hand. "And you? How are *you* today?"

Ruth placed her other hand over Katie's, giving her a reassuring smile. "I'm *gut* too. *Gott* has already covered me in His peace and assurance."

Katie's concern deepened, and her voice wavered as she pressed on. "But *Mamm*... cancer..."

Ruth shook her head firmly, cutting her off before she could finish. "*Nee*, we're not going to breathe life into that ugly word. *Gott* has this in His hands, and I won't allow worrisome thoughts to take root. I'm fully trusting in His healing power."

Katie's lips pressed together, her eyes glistening with unshed tears. "But *Mamm*, I just want to help. This morning, Susan Schrock was telling me about a doctor in Mexico. Her *schwester* started..."

"Stop," Ruth said calmly, her hand tightening around Katie's. "I don't want to hear about anyone else's journey right now. I need to keep my mind clear and uncluttered so I can hear *Gott's* instructions. His voice is the only one I'm listening for."

Katie wiped the corner of her eyes with the back of her hand, her shoulders sagging with the weight of helplessness. "I feel so useless. What can I do? How can I help you through this?"

Ruth's expression softened, and she tenderly cupped her daughter's cheek. "You have two hands and two knees, *jah*?"

Katie nodded; her eyes locked on her mother's.

"Then use them," Ruth said with a quiet, steady conviction. "Lift my name to the Lord in prayer. That's all the help I need."

Katie's lip trembled as she nodded, tears slipping down her cheeks. "I will. Every day."

Ruth smiled, a deep sense of peace radiating from her. "And that will be enough. We'll leave the rest in *Gott's* hands."

Emma's familiar voice followed the soft knock on the door as she stepped into the room, balancing a basket covered in a checkered cloth. "I thought I'd bring some fresh bread by. Figured you could use the help with the little ones running circles around you."

Katie smiled gratefully, rising from her chair to greet her

sister-in-law. "*Denki*. You're a lifesaver." She gestured toward the table. "Set it down and stay for a bit."

Emma's eyes brightened at Ruth sitting at the table. She set the basket on the table and made her way over, giving Ruth a quick hug. "Any news from the doctor yet?"

Ruth's smile was calm. "I meet with the surgeon tomorrow. He'll go over the options, suggest treatments, and we'll go from there, *jah*?"

Emma's brow furrowed in concern, her hands fidgeting with the hem of her apron. "That must be weighing heavily on you."

Ruth shook her head mildly. "I trust the Lord will give the doctor the wisdom we need. There's no sense in worrying about what we don't know yet."

Emma nodded. "You've always had such strong faith. I'll be praying. We all will."

Ruth smiled, the warmth of Emma's words settling in her heart. "*Denki*, Emma. That's all I ask."

***

After Ruth left to prepare dinner for Levi, the kitchen fell into a comfortable silence. Emma and Katie sat at the table, both lost in thought as the weight of their earlier conversation lingered in the air. Katie absently rubbed her belly, her mind swirling with concern for her mother.

Emma glanced over, noticing the quiet tension settling on Katie's face. "What's on your mind?"

Katie hesitated for a moment before speaking in a hushed tone. "I'm worried about *Mamm*. She's not talking about it, the diagnosis, I mean. I know she's trusting *Gott*, but it feels like she's not really letting any of us in. Like she's brushing it off, and I don't know how to help her." Her hand stilled on her belly, and her voice cracked as she continued. "I'm scared. Without her, I don't know how I'd get through this... this pregnancy, or this season of life."

Emma sighed, her own hands folding tightly in her lap. "I know what you mean. Your mother has always been there for all of us, hasn't she? But this... this has stirred up something I wasn't prepared for." Her voice faltered for a moment.

"What do you mean?" Katie asked.

Emma shifted in her chair, her eyes dropping to the table. "It's hard to separate what's happening now from what happened with my mother all those years ago." She paused, her voice thick with emotion. The fear, the helplessness... it's all coming back, and I'm struggling to keep the two apart. I know Ruth's situation is different, but it's hard not to relive some of that pain of losing my own mother to this awful disease."

Katie's eyes filled with tears as she reached across the table and grasped Emma's hand. "I didn't realize it was bringing back all those memories for you."

Emma nodded, blinking back her own tears. "It is. And it's hard because I want to be strong for her, for you, for everyone. But sometimes... sometimes it feels like I'm already grieving for something that hasn't even happened yet. And I hate that."

Katie's breath hitched as her own emotions bubbled to the surface. "I don't know what I'll do if... if she's not here to help me with the *kinner*. I don't even want to think about it, but it keeps creeping into my thoughts. I'm not ready to be without her."

Emma squeezed Katie's hand tightly. "I know. But we can't let those thoughts take over. *Mamm's* trusting *Gott*, and we have to do the same."

Katie wiped her tears with the back of her hand, nodding slowly. "I know you're right. It's just so hard to imagine life without her guiding us."

They sat silently for a moment, their hands still clasped, sharing the unspoken fear and love they both carried for Ruth.

***

Wilma stepped out of her car just as a white passenger van pulled up to the front entrance of the surgeon's office. Her eyes followed the van as it came to a stop, and a wave of recognition swept over her when she saw Ruth making her way around the vehicle. Ruth's familiar, warm smile greeted her, and Wilma couldn't help but feel a sense of comfort in seeing the Amish woman again.

"Fancy meeting you here," Wilma called out as she walked toward the door. Levi was already there, holding it open for both women with a courteous nod.

"I suspect we're both here for the same reason, *jah*?" Ruth responded gently; her eyes filled with quiet understanding.

"I reckon," Wilma replied with a half-hearted laugh, her voice betraying her nerves. "I'd just as soon get a tooth pulled, to tell the truth."

Ruth chuckled, her smile kind. "*Ach*, I don't think I'd go quite that far. But I can think of a hundred other things I'd rather be doing today."

The two women exchanged their information at the check-in desk and made their way to the waiting room, settling in next to each other. The sterile environment, with its muted colors and faint scent of disinfectant, felt anything but comforting.

The soft music playing in the background only heightened the sense of waiting... waiting for news, waiting for answers, waiting for their lives to shift in ways neither was quite prepared for.

Wilma leaned in closer to Ruth, her voice lowering. "I hope this doesn't take long. I've got a stack of papers to grade before I can call it a day."

Ruth raised an eyebrow. "Are you a schoolteacher?"

Wilma let out a small giggle, more nervous than amused. "If you can call it that. Most days, I feel more like a glorified babysitter."

Ruth's smile widened though there was a knowing glint in her eyes. "Children can be a handful. But they bring a lot of joy."

Wilma nodded, though her thoughts were elsewhere. Before she could respond, Ruth's name was called. Ruth stood, smoothing out her skirt, and smiled warmly at Wilma, her voice soft but steady. "I'll be praying for you."

Wilma's breath caught a little at the sincerity in Ruth's words. "Thanks."

Ruth gave her a final nod before walking toward the exam room with Levi by her side. His hand rested on the small of her back, guiding her with quiet strength. Wilma's eyes followed them, a pang of longing tightening in her chest. She instantly regretted not telling Seth about the appointment. But she'd brushed it off, just like she did with everything else... another problem to deal with later.

As she sat there, waiting for her name to be called, Ruth's words echoed in her mind. *Praying.* Wilma couldn't remember the last time she'd prayed. Life had a way of getting too busy, too noisy, and somewhere along the way, prayer had fallen by the wayside. In truth, she hadn't given much thought to prayer, or to faith, in years. It seemed like something for other people, like Ruth, who carried their faith so naturally, as if it was woven into the very fabric of their lives.

Wilma glanced around the room, her gaze settling on the peaceful expression Ruth had worn when they first met at the clinic. There was something about Ruth that felt different, a calmness, a quiet assurance that seemed to radiate from her, even in the face of something as terrifying as a cancer diagnosis. Was it her faith? Wilma had lived among the Amish her whole life, but she'd never really understood their way of life, their beliefs, or what gave them such strength in moments like this.

Religious status, Wilma thought wryly. *Is that a thing?* She'd never considered what it meant to rcly on something greater than herself. Her whole life, she'd pushed through challenges with sheer willpower and a good dose of sarcasm. But now, sitting in this cold, sterile waiting room, facing the uncertainty of her own health, she wondered if maybe Ruth had found something she hadn't.

For the first time in a long while, Wilma felt the faint stirrings of curiosity about faith. And maybe... just maybe... there was something to the peace Ruth seemed to carry with her, a peace that Wilma found herself wanting more than she'd ever expected.

***

The exam room was cold, and Ruth couldn't help but feel exposed and self-conscious in nothing but the flimsy paper gown. She tugged it tighter around her chest, her fingers fidgeting nervously.

Levi sat across from her, his expression full of concern. He reached for her hand, giving it a gentle squeeze. "Are you sure you wouldn't like to be alone for this exam?" he asked again.

Ruth shook her head, meeting his gaze. "*Nee,* I need you here with me. I'm afraid I won't remember everything the doctor says, or I might not understand it all. I need your ears more than my comfort right now."

Levi nodded, understanding her need for reassurance.

Within a few moments, the surgeon entered, politely introducing himself as he flipped through Ruth's chart. His demeanor was calm and professional, but Ruth could feel the weight of what was about to be discussed settling on her shoulders. She swallowed hard, trying to focus on his words.

"Ruth, I'm going to go over your scans and examine where the tumor cluster is located," the doctor explained. He placed the chart aside and instructed her to lay back on the exam table. Ruth's heart pounded in her chest as she complied, staring up at the ceiling as the surgeon's fingers lightly examined the area where the tumors had developed.

When the exam was over, the surgeon gave her time to sit up, and Levi draped her shawl over her shoulders. The warmth of the familiar fabric helped her relax, if only for a moment.

"Now, let's discuss your options," the surgeon began, settling into his chair across from them. He spoke clearly, but the terms swiftly became a jumble of long, complicated medical phrases that seemed foreign to Ruth's ears. The words blurred together, leaving Ruth struggling to focus.

She glanced over at Levi, who was busy scribbling down notes, trying to capture every detail. Ruth closed her eyes briefly, her silent prayer slipping from her lips in a scarcely audible whisper: *You are my God. You are with me. I will trust You in all things.*

As the surgeon paused to give them time to absorb the information, Ruth felt her mind swirling with uncertainty. Her eyes darted to Levi, hoping he would ask the questions she couldn't form. The lump in her throat made it impossible to speak.

The surgeon's voice broke through the haze. "Do either of you have any questions?"

Ruth looked at Levi, her eyes pleading for him to say something... anything... but he shook his head. His face was tight with concentration, but she knew he was overwhelmed too.

The surgeon nodded and continued, his tone compassionate but firm. "While I don't believe your diagnosis is life-threatening at this point, it's important not to delay your decision regarding treatment. I'll have my nurse provide you with everything we've discussed in writing so you can take it home and go through it at your own pace. This will give you the chance to make an informed choice."

Ruth felt a wave of relief as the conversation neared its end. When Levi stood to follow the doctor out of the room, she was grateful for the moment of privacy. Alone, she let out the breath she hadn't realized she'd been holding, her shoulders sagging as the tension slowly drained from her body. She whispered her breath prayer again, hoping to steady the anxiety that had crept into her heart with the onslaught of information.

"You are my strength, Lord," she whispered, closing her eyes briefly. *"And I find my peace in You."*

Ruth stood, her hands trembling a little as she smoothed out her clothes and prepared to leave. She opened the door quietly, her breath steady but her mind still reeling. The path ahead was uncertain, but she knew where her strength came from. *Gott* would guide her, just as He always had.

***

In a room two doors down from Ruth, Wilma sat alone, her fingers absentmindedly rubbing her bare shoulders beneath the thin hospital gown. The chill of the room clung to her skin, but it wasn't just the cold that made her shiver. Her mind felt numb, and her heart pounded in her chest, as if trying to keep pace with the flood of information being thrown at her.

The surgeon entered the room, followed by a nurse, but their presence felt distant, like figures in a dream she couldn't wake from. She watched the surgeon's mouth move, his words coming out in a steady stream, but they barely registered in her mind.

Mastectomy, chemotherapy, cancer prevention drugs for five years... the words echoed in her head like some nightmare, repeating themselves over and over again. She wanted to scream, to tell him to stop, but her voice felt trapped in her throat. He continued speaking, his tone calm, detached, almost rehearsed, probably the same speech he gave at least twenty times a day.

Wilma's breath quickened as the weight of it all bore down on her. This wasn't supposed to be her reality. This was supposed to happen to someone else. Someone older. Someone sicker. Not her. She was just thirty-three. She had so much of her life ahead of her. She wasn't ready for this. Not even close.

The nurse must have noticed the panic rising in her, because she stepped closer, placing a gentle hand on Wilma's arm. The touch was warm, a brief moment of humanity in the otherwise clinical atmosphere. But it wasn't enough to pull Wilma back from the edge.

"The diagnosis is severe," the surgeon said, his voice clear now, cutting through the fog in her mind. "Given the aggressiveness of the cancer, we'll need to move forward with your treatment as soon as possible. I suggest we start chemotherapy next week. We'll need to shrink your tumor before I can perform surgery."

Next week. The words hit Wilma like a punch to the gut, knocking the wind from her. Her options were limited, and time was running out. Everything felt like it was spinning out of control.

She stared at the surgeon, but it was as if she were looking through him, her mind a chaotic blur. She couldn't process it. Not now. Not here. She felt like she was falling, sinking into some abyss of fear and isolation. There was no Seth beside her, no one to hold her hand, no one to help her make sense of it all. The room seemed to close in around her, the walls pressing in, and she had never felt so utterly alone in her life.

The surgeon paused, giving her a moment, but his eyes were focused and professional. He had delivered this news so many times before. He had seen so many reactions... shock, fear, resignation. Wilma was just another patient to him, another case in a long line of difficult diagnoses. But to her, this was everything. This was her life, and it was crumbling around her.

"I know this is overwhelming," the nurse said kindly, her hand still resting on Wilma's arm. "Take a moment, and when you're ready, we'll discuss the next steps."

But Wilma didn't know if she'd ever be ready. The next steps seemed too huge, too insurmountable. She couldn't fathom it. All of it felt impossible to face.

CHAPTER 4

Ruth glanced out her kitchen window and watched a small group of her friends make their way up the driveway, their black shawls fluttering slightly in the breeze. She took a deep breath, drawing it deep into her chest, and prayed silently for the strength to be gracious. She knew they meant well, but the sight of them triggered a small warning in her heart. With every step they took toward her back door, she felt a familiar tug of unease. She wasn't looking for pity or fear. What she needed... what she had resolved to cling to... was faith.

A light knock interrupted her thoughts, and she turned just as Susan's head peeked inside the door. "Ruth, it's Susan. Are you too busy for a surprise visit?"

Ruth forced a genuine smile and waved them in. "*Ach,* please come in. It's always a bright day when friends come a-calling."

Susan removed her shawl, hanging it on the peg by the back

door, and the two other women followed her inside. They settled around the kitchen table as if they had done it a thousand times before. Ruth busied herself by retrieving four clean cups from the cupboard. "I baked a batch of banana muffins this morning," she said casually. "The good Lord must have known I'd have special visitors today."

Susan, already seated, eyed the sugar bowl and pulled it closer in anticipation of the fresh coffee. "I thought I smelled something sweet when I walked in the door," she said with a grin.

"So, what do I owe this wonderful visit to?" Ruth asked, pouring the coffee as the rich aroma filled the kitchen.

Susan exchanged a glance with the two women across the table before speaking. "We came to check on you. To see how we can help you through this... awful season."

Ruth paused, her chin tilting slightly as she processed Susan's words. "Awful season?" she repeated. "I'm not sure what you mean."

Susan shifted in her seat as she added two heaping teaspoons of sugar to her cup. "Now, Ruth, we all know about your diagnosis. You don't have to hide your true emotions or anxiety from us. We're here to walk with you through this, every step of the way. That's what friends do."

Ruth kept her voice steady, though she felt a prickling unease at Susan's words. "I certainly appreciate your concern, but honestly, I'm not worried or anxious."

Susan let out a soft gasp, her spoon pausing mid-stir. "*Ach*, Ruth, but it's cancer. My aunt went through the same thing, and she... she lost..."

Ruth's hand stilled as she firmly placed the coffee pot back on the stove. "Please, Susan," she interrupted, her voice gentle but resolute. "I'd rather not hear about anyone else's journey. Here, in my home, we're speaking words of faith. I trust the Lord to direct my path, and I won't give power to fear or worry. I'm leaning on His promises."

The room fell into a brief, uneasy silence as Ruth's words hung in the air. She watched as the three women exchanged glances, their concern obvious.

"But Ruth," Susan persisted, "you must be practical. You need to plan and explore all your options. That's just being responsible."

Ruth took her time before responding, her heart steady in her conviction. She sat down at the table beside Susan, her eyes meeting her friend's. "Susan, I appreciate your concern, truly.

But I'm choosing to keep my eyes on the Lord. I'm praying, reading His Word, and praising Him for His faithfulness. I believe He won't forget me, and I'm waiting on Him to work a miracle."

The tension in the room was visible as her friends struggled to reconcile Ruth's unwavering faith with their own fear for her. Ruth could see the confusion and concern etched on their faces, but she refused to waver. She reached for the platter of muffins and passed it around the table with a calm smile.

"The words we speak have power," Ruth said as the muffins made their way around the table. "And here, we're going to speak words that are filled with faith."

Her friends nodded, though their eyes still held traces of uncertainty. But Ruth remained firm, her heart anchored in the knowledge that her journey would be guided by the One she trusted most.

***

A ray of sunshine landed on the stack of test papers on Wilma's counter. Normally, her Saturday mornings were for unwinding... taking a long walk, stopping at *The Sandwich*

Shoppe for her favorite chocolate hazelnut coffee. But today? Today felt like she was living in some alternate reality, one where her future had become a tangled mess of medical terms and unwanted decisions.

Her phone vibrated on the counter again. She glanced at it, saw both Seth's and Janel's missed calls, and promptly ignored them. The last thing she had energy for was talking about her diagnosis. No, what she really needed was her normal Saturday routine: a walk, her favorite coffee, and pretending everything was fine.

Grabbing her sneakers and sweatshirt, she stepped out onto the sidewalk, almost colliding with a couple of Amish women coming out of *The Mercantile*. "Pardon me," Wilma said quickly, offering them a polite smile. "Do either of you know where I might find Ruth Yoder's house?"

The women exchanged cautious glances and spoke something in Pennsylvania Dutch to each other before one answered hesitantly, "That would be Levi's Ruth. They live out at *Yoder's Strawberry Acres*, behind the bakery on Mystic Mill Road."

Wilma flashed a grateful smile, internally relieved they hadn't thought her request too strange. "Thank you so much," she said brightly, mentally noting Ruth's location before setting off toward Willow Springs Park.

No sooner had she made it to her favorite part of the path when her phone vibrated again. This time, she answered Janel's call.

"It's about time you picked up! I was about to send a search party!" Janel's voice came through the phone, half-joking but with a layer of genuine concern.

"Sorry, sorry," Wilma said, forcing a laugh. "I've been busy trying to figure out how to keep all my body parts attached, you know, the usual."

Janel didn't laugh. "Wilma, how did the appointment go?"

Wilma shifted her weight, her sarcasm bubbling up as her defense mechanism. "Oh, you know, all the fun stuff. Lots of medical jargon that no one understands except the guy in green surgical clothes. But the short version? I'm about to lose two rather large and, might I add, fabulous parts of my anatomy."

"Wilma!" Janel gasped, her concern deepening.

"What?" Wilma countered; her voice flippant. "I mean, sure, they're planning to cut off half of what makes me look great in a dress, but hey, maybe I'll start a new trend... *flat is the new fabulous.*"

Janel sighed, clearly trying to keep up with Wilma's banter but not quite succeeding. "I'm so sorry. When's the surgery?"

Wilma leaned against a bench, rolling her eyes even though Janel couldn't see. "Not for awhile. Seems they need to shrink things first. I go in next week to get some sort of port put in and then they're fast-tracking me. Gotta love efficiency in healthcare, right?"

"And Seth?" Janel's voice softened. "How's he taking it?" Wilma hesitated, her humor faltering for a moment. "Yeah, about that... I haven't exactly told him yet."

"What?" Janel's voice spiked with disbelief. "You haven't told him? Wilma, he deserves to know!"

Wilma flopped onto the bench, throwing her free hand in the air. "Janel, come on. What am I supposed to say? 'Hey, Seth, guess what! In a few months, I'll be minus two body parts, and we may or may not get a happily ever after?' That's not exactly romantic."

"You're making jokes, but this is serious, Wilma," Janel replied. "You can't make this decision for him. Seth loves you, and he deserves to know what's going on."

"Yeah, well, love isn't exactly chemotherapy-proof, is it?" Wilma shot back, the humor still on her lips, but her heart squeezing painfully. "He wants a family, kids. How can I give him all that when I'm not even sure I'll be around to... you know... finish the job?"

Janel was quiet for a moment, and when she spoke again, her voice was gentle but unyielding. "Wilma, you're not giving Seth a chance to decide for himself. You're deciding for him. You don't know what he'll say until you tell him."

Wilma stared at the ground, tapping her foot. "I just... I don't want to drag him through this mess. Who wants to watch their girlfriend turn into a walking episode of *Grey's Anatomy*?"

"Maybe he wants to be there for you," Janel suggested. "Maybe he'll surprise you. But you won't know unless you're honest with him."

Wilma sighed, leaning her head back against the bench. "Yeah, well, let's just say it's a little hard to lead with, 'Hey, honey, I'm about to lose my boobs and possibly my sanity. How do you feel about that?'"

Janel let out a soft laugh, but her concern remained. "You'll find the right words, Wilma. Just... don't wait too long. Seth deserves to know."

Wilma didn't answer right away. Instead, she sat there in the park, feeling the weight of Janel's words pressing on her heart. She knew her friend was right. But facing that conversation... facing Seth... felt like opening a door she wasn't ready to step through just yet.

"I'll think about it," Wilma said, her voice quieter now.

"Good," Janel replied, her voice softening. "Just remember, you're not alone in this, okay? I'm here. Seth's there. Let us in."

Wilma nodded, even though Janel couldn't see her. "Thanks, Janel. I'll talk to you soon."

As she hung up, Wilma leaned forward, resting her elbows on her knees. She stared down at her phone, the screen dark and silent, and wondered just how long she could keep pretending everything was fine.

***

Later that afternoon, it was unusually noisy at the bookstore below Wilma's upstairs apartment, and she found it nearly impossible to concentrate on the stack of test papers spread across the kitchen island. She had been trying to drown out the world with her work, but the constant noise from the store and the nagging thoughts in her mind weren't helping. She glanced at the clock just as Seth knocked carelessly on her door and stepped inside.

"Hey. You had me worried. You haven't answered my calls all day," Seth said, his voice carrying a tad of frustration.

Wilma looked up, feeling a flash of embarrassment but masking it with a half-hearted smile. She waved her hand over the chaotic pile of papers in front of her. "Yeah, I've been a little busy. You know, wrangling my students' grammar mistakes and wondering how any of them will survive in the real world."

Seth moved closer, wrapping his arm around her waist and pulling her against him. "Too busy for me?" he teased, pressing a tender kiss to her forehead.

Feeling somewhat suffocated by the sudden affection, Wilma smoothly pushed him away, her heart tightening with the secret she was keeping. "End of the grading period," she said, forcing a casual tone as she motioned to the papers.

Seth didn't seem to take the hint. He pulled out a stool and sat down beside her at the island, his expression softening. But Wilma could see it; the telltale clench of his jaw. She knew him well enough to recognize when he was disappointed, even if he didn't say it outright.

"You forgot we had a date this afternoon," Seth finally said.

Wilma ran a hand through her uncombed hair, feeling the mess of her haphazard attire... an oversized sweater and mismatched socks. She exhaled sharply. "Uh... yeah, about that. Can I take a rain check? I've got about a million things to do before Monday, and unless these papers grade themselves, I'm not going anywhere."

Seth stood; his frustration now visible as he started stacking her papers into neat piles. "Nope, I'm not letting you off the hook. You've put me off for two weeks now, and today is the day I get you out of this apartment, even if I have to carry you out kicking and screaming."

Wilma raised an eyebrow, her snark already bubbling to the surface. "Really? Kicking and screaming, huh?"

Ignoring her sarcasm, Seth grabbed a few more papers and stacked them methodically. "You need a break. I'm serious, Wilma. You're working yourself into the ground, and I'm not taking no for an answer."

Wilma moved behind him, separating the papers back into her scattered mess. "I don't have time for this, Seth. I need to get these graded before I go..." She stopped mid-sentence, catching herself.

Seth's eyes narrowed, catching her slip-up. "Before you go

where?"

"Nowhere," Wilma snapped, her voice defensive. She didn't like where this was heading. "I just don't have time for a break today."

Seth wasn't so easily deterred. Without warning, he scooped her up and carried her, despite her half-hearted protests. "Seth! What are you doing?" she exclaimed, half-laughing but fully annoyed.

"You leave me no choice." He plopped her down on her bed with a grin, then pointed toward her closet. "Give me four hours, and I'll have you back here in plenty of time to finish grading. But we're going out, and you need to dress warmly. Jeans, sweatshirt, and no arguing."

He left the room before she could argue, shutting the door behind him with a finality that left Wilma sitting on her bed, frazzled and a tad bit irritated by his bossy attitude. She flopped back onto the mattress, staring up at the ceiling.

"Great," she muttered to herself. "Apparently, I'm dating a man who moonlights as a drill sergeant."

She sighed, staring up at the ceiling. The sarcasm had come easy, as it always did when she felt cornered, but beneath it all, there was something else... something heavier. Seth's persistence was frustrating but also comforting in a way she didn't want to acknowledge. He didn't give up on her, even when she was at her snappiest, even when she threw up walls to keep him at a distance.

As much as she wanted to push him away, part of her wondered if she should just tell him the truth, the real reason she'd been avoiding him, why she couldn't focus, why everything felt so... fragile. Could she really burden him with that?

Wilma closed her eyes, her chest tightening with indecision. She knew she couldn't keep up this act forever, but the thought of seeing his face when she told him... when the weight of what she was carrying finally came crashing down... was almost too much to bear.

***

Wilma closed her eyes, letting the warmth of the sun seep into her skin as Seth drove them out of town and onto I-79 North. The rolling hills of green stretched out in front of them, a peaceful backdrop to a day she hadn't planned but was trying to embrace. Keeping her eyes on the scenery, she turned to Seth with a playful smirk. "So, where exactly are you dragging me off to, kidnapper?"

Seth motioned with his head toward the backseat. "I packed a picnic, grabbed a couple of fishing poles, and thought we'd head out to Woodcock Dam for a couple of hours."

Wilma's lips curled into a genuine smile. *Woodcock Dam,* she thought. It was one of her favorite spots... quiet, peaceful, and tucked away from the world. "Fishing and a picnic? You sure know how to woo a girl," she teased, reaching back to flip the lid on the picnic basket. "What culinary masterpiece did you prepare for us today?"

Seth rapidly swatted her hand away, chuckling. "Oh no you don't. I'd hate for you to spill the worms all over the fried chicken and coleslaw I picked up."

Wilma gasped dramatically, her hands flying to her chest in mock horror. "Worms? Fried chicken? Oh, Seth, you know the way to a woman's heart," she said, fluttering her eyelashes and giving her best impression of a Southern belle. "Why, I do declare, nightcrawlers and greasy chicken are all I ever dreamed of."

Seth laughed, shaking his head at her antics as he turned on the radio. "You're ridiculous."

"I try," Wilma replied, settling back into her seat, her smile lingering. She was doing her best to play the part... the fun, carefree girlfriend who wasn't secretly hiding with life-altering news. She could feel the tension in her shoulders loosening, even if just for a moment.

Less than thirty minutes later, Seth pulled his truck into a parking spot at the base of the dam. The park was buzzing with early spring enthusiasm, as locals embraced the sun-filled day after a long, unforgiving northwestern Pennsylvania winter. The air was fresh, and the sound of children laughing and birds chirping echoed around them.

Wilma looped her arm through Seth's as they strolled toward a vacant picnic table, the sun warming their faces. "Do you want to eat first or fish?" Seth asked, his voice light but carrying a hint of something else... something she couldn't quite place.

"I'd say let's eat first. The smell of that chicken is making my stomach growl," she replied with a playful grin.

Seth grunted in mock warning. "I've seen you devour fried chicken before. Let me get mine first this time."

Wilma raised an eyebrow, her lips curling into a smirk. "What are you trying to say?"

He nudged her playfully with his hip, moving her away from the picnic basket. "I'm just saying I want first dibs on the best piece, that's all."

She threw her hands up in exaggerated protest, giggling. "Fine! Have at it, greedy."

They both laughed, their easy banter filling the space between them. A soft breeze flickered across Wilma's face, and she felt Seth's gentle hand move a strand of hair from her mouth as she took her first bite of crispy chicken.

"Yum," she moaned, savoring the crunch. "This is heavenly."

Seth chuckled; his eyes soft as he watched her. "You sure do love your food."

"What's not to love?" she teased, licking a bit of grease from her fingers. "Honestly, I think I love fried chicken more than almost anything else in the world."

Seth raised an eyebrow, a mischievous smile tugging at his lips. "More than me?"

Wilma didn't miss a beat, grinning as she replied, "Right at this moment, while I'm sinking my teeth into this crispy, spicy goodness? Absolutely."

They both laughed, the tension in the air feeling light and

playful. But as the meal wound down, and Seth began pulling out the container of worms and retrieving his tackle box from the truck, Wilma felt a shift. Something deeper was brewing beneath the surface.

Following him to the small winding creek at the base of the dam, Wilma busied herself with rigging her fishing rod just as he'd taught her, the familiar activity offering a sense of normalcy. But then Seth's voice broke through her focus.

"I think you've graduated into putting your own worm on the hook now," Seth teased, but his tone was softer, almost tender.

Wilma rolled her eyes, playfully grimacing. "Really? That's the part I hate the most."

Seth crouched down beside her, setting his fishing pole on the ground. For a moment, she thought he was just tying his shoe. But then he handed her the container of worms, his hand lingering a little longer than usual.

She glanced at him curiously. "What's this? You're really making me do this?"

When Seth didn't respond immediately, her eyes narrowed in suspicion. Something about the way he was looking at her, hopeful, expectant, made her heart race. She took the container and flipped the lid open.

Inside, instead of a pile of wriggling nightcrawlers, she found a delicate diamond ring, resting on top of glittering gold confetti. Her breath caught in her throat, her eyes widening in disbelief.

For a split second, her mind whirled with a thousand thoughts. She saw Seth kneeling in front of her, his hopeful smile lighting up his face. She saw the ring, the symbol of a future he clearly wanted with her. But alongside that vision came another... one of hospitals, surgeries, chemo... a future far more uncertain than she could bear to think about.

Her heart pounded as the weight of it all crashed over her. This wasn't the fairytale moment she should've been dreaming about. This was a nightmare. How could she accept a future she wasn't even sure she'd be part of?

When Seth ultimately spoke, his voice was soft, filled with hope. "Wilma, will you marry me?"

Wilma's lips trembled as she stared at him, her mind screaming with uncertainty. The visions of what could be, the life he wanted and the reality she faced collided in her head. A million reasons why this wouldn't work flooded her thoughts, none of them leading to a happy ending.

She shook her head, unable to find the words. "Seth, I... I can't."

75

CHAPTER 5

The quiet morning gave Ruth the time she needed to tend to her flower gardens before Levi came in for their noon meal. Little pockets of weeds had started to pop up between the blooming tulips and daffodils, and Ruth smiled as the freshly turned earth framed the colorful flowers in a perfect, dark border. She knelt, brushing the soil from her hands, when the crunch of tires on the gravel drive reached her ears.

Ruth straightened, turning toward the driveway just as a sleek silver car pulled up to the house. The car's gleaming surface was unmistakable, and Ruth recognized the young woman from the surgeon's office... *Wilma,* she recalled. What could have brought her all the way out here?

Wiping her brow with the back of her hand, Ruth waved as Wilma stepped out of the car, her expression both hopeful and uncertain.

"What a wonderful surprise," Ruth called warmly, making

her way over to greet her. "Wilma, it's good to see you again!"

Wilma smiled, though it was tinged with a hint of apprehension. "I hope you don't mind me just dropping by. I asked a couple of women in town this morning where I could find your place. I wasn't sure if it was too forward..."

"Heavens, no, child," Ruth said, her voice full of reassurance. "Please, come inside. You're more than welcome." Ruth led Wilma around the side of the house to the kitchen door, motioning for her to sit at the table as she moved toward the stove. "Tea or coffee?" she asked, already pulling out two cups.

"Coffee is fine," Wilma replied, taking in her surroundings. "But you don't have to go to any trouble. I was just hoping to talk for a few minutes if you have the time."

Ruth chuckled slightly as she poured the coffee. "Oh, I have plenty of time these days. My family's been taking most of the work off my hands since, well, you know. Besides, with no little ones running around anymore, this house stays much cleaner than it used to."

Wilma glanced around the kitchen, her eyes lingering on the warm, homey touches. "It's so welcoming in here. Simple, but... comforting."

Ruth smiled, pouring herself a cup of green tea. "It's

different from the *Englisch* kitchens, I'm sure."

"Actually," Wilma replied, wrapping her hands around the warm mug, "I live above the *Book Cellar*, so my apartment is simple too. It used to belong to an Amish family, so I've grown to appreciate the simplicity."

Ruth nodded, understanding. Simplicity had a way of bringing peace, especially in times of uncertainty. "How did your appointment go last week?" Ruth asked, her voice soft with concern.

Wilma sighed, her chin resting in her hand. "Honestly? It was information overload. I could hardly keep track of half of what they were saying."

Ruth gave an understanding nod. "I felt the same way at my appointment. I was thankful Levi was there taking notes. Otherwise, I don't think I would have remembered half of it."

"Will you need surgery?" Wilma asked, her voice tentative.

"That's a decision I'll need to make soon," Ruth admitted. "But for now, I'm praying and waiting for guidance from the Lord."

She noticed the way Wilma's brow furrowed considerably, but the younger woman didn't ask for more details. Ruth decided to let it be, sensing that Wilma had more pressing things on her mind. "And you?" Ruth asked.

Wilma took a deep breath before answering, her fingers tracing the rim of her mug. "The type of cancer I have... it grows really fast. Triple-negative, they called it. I'm still trying to wrap my head around all the medical terms. The treatment's going to be aggressive, though. Surgery, chemo... the whole nine yards."

Ruth's heart sank at the weight of Wilma's words. The young woman had such a difficult road ahead. "Do you have family here in Willow Springs?" Ruth asked, hoping to gauge the support Wilma might have.

"My father's still around," Wilma replied, her voice soft. "But his health isn't the best. He's in a memory care unit, and, well, he's not really able to be there for me like he used to be. My mom passed away when I was a teenager, so it's mostly just me now." She hesitated, then added, "I do have a boyfriend, but... I haven't told him yet."

Ruth felt a pang of sadness for the young woman. It wasn't her place to pry, but she couldn't help but ask, "You haven't told him? Why not, if you don't mind me asking?"

Wilma sighed, her fingers tightening around her mug. "He's building up his remodeling business, and I just... I don't want to burden him with all this. He's got enough on his plate."

"How long have you been with him?" Ruth asked, her curiosity getting the better of her.

"Four years," Wilma answered, her voice soft.

"*Ach*, that's a long time. I'm sure he's very special to you, *jah*?"

"He is," Wilma admitted. "He's ready for more. Something more permanent. But with all this happening, it's just not the right time to think about the future."

Ruth considered her response carefully. She didn't want to push Wilma, but she could tell the young woman was struggling with more than just her diagnosis. "Sometimes," Ruth said kindly, "those we love are the ones who can help us through the hardest times. You don't have to carry this alone."

Wilma looked up, her eyes meeting Ruth's. For a moment, she seemed to consider Ruth's words, but then, just as quickly, she changed the subject. Ruth could see she wasn't ready to share more yet, and that was fine. They had time.

Wilma didn't quite understand why she had been drawn to Ruth, but something about the older woman's calm presence had tugged at her. It was as though Ruth radiated a peace that

Wilma desperately needed to grasp... a peace Wilma couldn't find in her own storm of thoughts. Ruth's voice had the warmth of a soft blanket, and the stillness of her kitchen soothed the chaos in Wilma's mind. Taking a long sip from her cup, Wilma gathered enough nerve to ask the questions that had been gnawing at her since her diagnosis.

"I know we barely know each other," Wilma began, her words coming out slowly, "but I don't really have anyone else who might understand what's going through my head these last few days."

Ruth smiled, her hands cradling her cup of tea. "*Ach*, I imagine our thoughts have been swirling around some of the same uncertainties, *jah*?"

"Yeah, you might say that," Wilma replied, her fingers tracing the rim of her mug. She hesitated, then gestured vaguely over her chest. "Mine are more about losing these." Her bluntness made Ruth's cheeks flush a soft pink, and Wilma winced, promptly backtracking. "I'm sorry. Sometimes my mouth runs ahead of me before I've thought things through."

Ruth nodded, her smile never wavering. "I'm just not used to such bold discussions," she admitted, her tone more curious than offended. "It's not typically our way."

Wilma let out a small laugh. "Yeah, whoops. I guess I tend to overshare sometimes. My dad used to tell me to think twice before I speak. Clearly, I never really learned that lesson."

Wilma had never spoken to an Amish woman this personally before. Sure, she lived in the same town, passed them in the stores or along the roads, but the Amish mostly kept to themselves. She could only imagine that Ruth might find her a bit... *much*.

But Ruth, ever gracious, placed a gentle hand on the table between them. "Don't stop being you, Wilma. We come from different worlds, *jah*, but that doesn't mean *Gott* didn't orchestrate our paths to cross... even through something like this." Ruth gestured jokingly across her own chest; her face soft with understanding. Both women chuckled, the tension between them easing for a moment.

Wilma's smile faded slightly as she spoke again, her voice quieter. "It's just... I never thought I'd be facing something like losing parts of my body. Important parts." Her voice wavered. "How's anyone supposed to deal with that?"

Ruth remained quiet for a moment, considering the weight of the question. "I suppose that's something we need to seek from the Lord for clarity," she said thoughtfully.

Wilma leaned in; her eyes filled with the desperation for answers she didn't yet have. "But you haven't thought about it? I mean, what it would feel like to lose something that's been part of you your whole life?"

Ruth looked at her attentively before responding, her voice steady but filled with faith. "No, I guess I haven't thought about it that way. But I don't believe losing them would make me any less of a woman in *Gott's* eyes."

Wilma swallowed hard, the words stirring something deep within her. "But what about in your husband's eyes? I mean... What if he doesn't see you the same way?"

Ruth paused, her cup resting in her hands. For a split second, she seemed to struggle with how to respond. But then, her faith spoke louder than any hesitation. "If that's the case," she began, her voice calm, "I'll trust that the Lord will work on Levi's heart, just as He's worked on mine."

Wilma sat back, absorbing Ruth's words. The certainty in Ruth's tone, the trust she placed so completely in God's plan... it was foreign to her but comforting.

The silence between them lingered, thick with unspoken fears and questions. Wilma's heart pounded as the weight of her thoughts pressed harder against her chest. She hadn't come here just to visit. No, there was something much deeper, something clawing at her insides that she couldn't contain any longer.

"I'm scared," she whispered, barely able to hear herself over the clock's ticking. Saying it out loud felt like tearing open a wound she'd been desperately trying to ignore. *There. I said it.* She took a quick glance at Ruth, worried her words might have been too blunt, too raw. But when she met Ruth's eyes, all she saw was calm—a calm she longed to feel herself.

For a moment, Ruth didn't say anything, and Wilma braced herself for whatever kind of response might follow. But there was no judgment in Ruth's eyes, no discomfort at Wilma's bold admission. Ruth's hand was warm and steady on the table between them, and that simple connection felt like an anchor in the storm swirling inside Wilma's mind.

When Ruth finally spoke, her voice was gentle, soothing. "*Ach*, it's only natural to feel fear when the future is so uncertain. But the peace you're searching for, that sense of calm in the storm? It can only come from one place. Ultimately, *Gott* is in control."

Wilma's stomach twisted. She wanted to believe that. She wanted to find comfort in the idea that there was a greater plan, that she didn't have to bear the weight of it all. But how could she let go when she'd spent her whole life holding everything together?

"What if I'm not strong enough to handle it?" Wilma's voice cracked, the vulnerability in her question surprising her. "What if I don't make it through this? What if... I'm not ready to die?"

The words tumbled out before she could stop them, her deepest fear laid bare between them. The admission tasted bitter on her tongue... she hated the weakness in it, hated how exposed it made her feel.

Ruth reached across the table, tapping her fingers delicately on Wilma's hand. The warmth of her touch, the steady presence of her calm, felt like a balm against Wilma's raw edges. "You don't have to be strong all the time," Ruth said. "That's the beauty of faith. It's not about us being strong enough. It's about leaning on *Gott* when we feel weak."

Wilma swallowed; her throat tight. She'd never been one to lean on anyone, let alone something as intangible as faith. "But I've never been... religious," she admitted. "I don't even know how to pray."

Ruth's smile was gentle, understanding. "You don't need to know the right words. You can start with what you just told me… 'I'm scared, Lord.' That's enough. He knows your heart."

Wilma stared at her, feeling a strange mix of disbelief and hope welling up inside. *Could it really be that simple? Just... tell God she was scared? No grand prayers, no perfect words, just... honesty?*

"I don't know if I can let go like that," Wilma whispered, her voice scarcely audible. "I've spent my whole life trying to be strong. Trying to handle things on my own."

Ruth's tipped her chin toward her. "Letting go doesn't mean giving up. It just means trusting that you don't have to carry this burden alone."

***

Ruth stood on the top step of the porch, her hand raised in farewell as Wilma's car disappeared down Mystic Mill Road. She watched until the car was out of sight, her heart aching for the young woman who had shared her fears so openly. Wilma's visit had left a deep impression on Ruth, and she couldn't help but feel the weight of it.

She prayed silently, hoping that her words had provided some measure of comfort, that Wilma would find peace in the midst of her struggle. But as the warm midday sun kissed Ruth's cheeks, she felt the familiar tug of her own uncertainties. She had been so sure, so confident in the Lord's faithfulness when speaking with Wilma. But now, in the quiet, the reality of her own situation settled heavily on her shoulders.

Sitting down in one of the rockers, Ruth allowed herself a rare moment of vulnerability. She let a few tears fall, her heart heavy with the unknown path ahead of her. She, too, was walking into uncharted territory, and though she trusted the Lord, that didn't mean the journey was free from fear.

"Lord," she whispered, her voice soft in the stillness of the room. "Show me the path that will bring You the most glory in this season. Help me to trust You, even when I'm scared. And please, let me be a light for Wilma as she searches for her own way through this."

The weight of her own diagnosis pressed against her, but Ruth knew that no matter what came, *Gott* was with her. That was her anchor, the faith that kept her steady, even when the storm raged. And as she sat there, the warmth of the sun still on her skin, Ruth felt a quiet assurance that she was not alone. God had never failed her before, and He wouldn't fail her now.

She wiped her eyes, straightened her back, and whispered

one final prayer. "Help me shine Your light, Lord, for both Wilma and me."

With that, Ruth rose from the rocker, determined to face the days ahead with the same unwavering faith she had always carried, and to be a source of comfort for Wilma, no matter what fears lay in her own heart.

***

The new day arrived with fresh news, and Ruth's heart swelled as Daniel appeared at the door, a beaming smile on his face. "Katie delivered a new little farmhand last night," he announced proudly.

"Daniel, why didn't you wake us?" Ruth's voice was a mix of joy and concern, her mind racing with thoughts of holding her new grandson.

"Katie felt you needed your rest," Daniel replied, his tone soft but firm. "The midwife had everything under control. But now that the girls are up, I could use a little extra help."

Ruth was already moving, placing her cup in the sink as she hurried up the stairs. "I'll be over in a split second," she called, already imagining the feel of her new grandson in her arms. "I'll get the girls settled and check on Katie."

Levi followed her, his face etched with concern. "Are you sure you should be doing so much?" he asked, his hand resting on her arm. "You've been running yourself ragged lately."

Ruth paused, sighing as she turned to face him. "Levi, please. This coddling is getting old. I'm perfectly capable of taking care of the girls and tending to Katie for a few days. I need to stay busy."

But Levi wasn't letting it go. He reached for her hand, pulling her tenderly down to sit beside him on the bed. "Ruth," his voice was softer now, more serious. "We haven't even discussed what we're going to tell the surgeon the day after tomorrow. Don't you think we should be making some decisions about your treatment plan?"

Ruth felt the weight of his words settle heavily on her chest, but she wasn't ready… not yet. She met his gaze, her fingers tightening around his. "Please, Levi, not now. Katie needs me. Let's talk about this later."

Levi squeezed her hand, his eyes filled with both love and worry. "Ruth, I know you want to be there for Katie, but this is important. We need to know where we stand with your health."

Ruth looked away for a moment, her thoughts swirling. She

wasn't ignoring the urgency of her own situation, but the timing felt... off. The joy of new life had come into their family, and she didn't want to taint that moment with heavy conversations about her health.

"I've been thinking about it," Ruth admitted calmly, her hand covering his. "I've been praying, asking *Gott* to show me what He wants me to do. And I do have some thoughts, but... can't we discuss it later? Right now, I just want to go meet our grandson."

Levi's shoulders relaxed a tad, though the worry didn't fully leave his eyes. "Alright," he replied. "But we'll talk about this later, *jah*? We can't put it off much longer."

Ruth nodded, giving him a small, reassuring smile. "Later," she promised, standing and smoothing her dress. "Now let's go meet our newest little one."

***

Katie and Daniel's home was brimming with joy. Little Daniel Jr. had arrived overnight, and by mid-morning, the entire family had found their way to their home. The house buzzed with excitement as one family member after another took turns cradling the newest addition to their family.

Ruth stood back for a moment, watching as Levi held the tiny boy in his large, calloused hands, a look of pure tenderness on his face. Otto and Owen, the twins, circled around, curious but quiet, while Ella and Mary giggled in the corner, making up stories about their new baby *bruder*. The warmth of family filled the room, letting Ruth get lost in the joy of the moment.

As she moved toward the couch where Katie rested, Ruth felt a sudden quietness settle over her heart. The laughter and chatter of the room seemed to fade, and in that stillness, she felt it—an unmistakable presence. It wasn't audible, yet the words were as clear as day in her heart: *"I'm not done with you yet, little soldier."*

The peace that followed those words was unlike anything Ruth had felt since her diagnosis. It was a deep, abiding rest, as though the heavy weight she'd been carrying was lifted in an instant. She knew, without a doubt, that *Gott* had spoken. His message was clear. *He wasn't done with her yet.*

That night, as she returned home after the day's celebrations, Ruth lay beside Levi in their bed. The moonlight filtering through the curtains. She snuggled her head on his shoulder, unconsciously placing her hand on his chest.

"I've made a decision," she whispered.

Levi shifted, laying a hand over hers. "*Ach*, what is it?"

She hesitated for just a moment, gathering her thoughts. "I've decided I'll go forward with the mastectomy. It's the best way to rid my body of these tumors... but after that," her voice faltered, "I don't know yet. I'll wait for *Gott's* direction before I make any other decisions."

Levi was silent for a moment, absorbing her words before he spoke. "I believe you're doing what's best. But I need you to know something."

Ruth turned her head slightly, meeting his eyes in the dim light.

"This surgery," Levi continued, his voice deep with emotion, "it doesn't make you any less of a woman. Not to me."

Ruth blinked, feeling a few tears slip down her cheeks. She had been so afraid—afraid of the surgery, afraid of losing a part of herself, afraid of how it would change things between them. But Levi's words, spoken with such love and tenderness, melted away those fears.

Levi reached over, wiping her tears away with the back of his hand. "It's just a single step on your path that the Lord has laid before you."

Ruth closed her eyes, letting the warmth of his words settle in her heart. She felt safe, knowing that Levi's love wasn't dependent on anything physical, and more importantly, that *Gott's* plan for her was still unfolding. She took a deep breath, her hand tightening around his. "Thank you," she whispered.

CHAPTER 6

Wilma tucked her legs up under herself, pulling the soft throw from the back of the sofa to cover her lap. She needed Janel's grounding presence, even if it was just through the phone. Dialing her number, she took a deep breath as her friend's familiar voice answered.

"Hey! Do you have a few minutes? I could really use some sound advice. My head's all over the place, and I need you to talk me off the ledge before I jump out of my skin."

"Of course," Janel replied warmly. "What's got you all worked up... besides the big elephant in the room?"

Wilma let out a weary laugh. "Oh, this isn't a little white elephant. It's the big, blindingly pink kind, with the gaudiest ribbon you've ever seen wrapped around it."

Janel chuckled, though Wilma could hear her friend's concern through the humor. "So, tell me—what's going on?"

"It's... everything," Wilma sighed, trying to keep her voice steady. "Seth, work... and they've scheduled chemo to start next week. I keep trying to make snide jokes to cover it all up, but honestly, I'm just overwhelmed."

There was a pause before Janel's gentle voice filled the line.

"Okay, let's start with Seth. How's he handling all this?"

Wilma hesitated, pressing her fingers to her forehead. "I... haven't told him."

Janel's gasp was audible. "What? Wilma, it's been weeks. Why haven't you told him?"

"I don't know. Maybe I just don't want to burden him with all this. He's got his business, his plans... and then there's me and my mess."

Janel was silent for a beat, then spoke in her no-nonsense tone. "You know I love you, but you're being grossly unfair. Seth deserves to know, and if you don't tell him, I'll find him myself and let him know what's going on."

"You wouldn't!" Wilma snapped.

"Oh, I would. He needs to make his own decisions, Wilma. It's not fair for you to decide what's best for him without even talking to him."

Wilma shifted the phone to her other ear, pulling her knees closer to her chest. The thought of seeing disappointment, or worse, pity, in Seth's eyes gnawed at her. After a long pause, she admitted softly, "He proposed last week."

A squeal came through the phone, causing Wilma to smile despite herself. "He proposed! Wilma, that's wonderful! All the more reason for you to tell him what's going on."

"But that's just it," Wilma murmured. "It's all too much at once. I had to take medical leave from work, and I told Seth I couldn't marry him. And now I have to face a mastectomy, a massive amount of chemo, losing my hair, reconstructive surgery, and who knows what else. My life is spinning out of control, like that carnival ride you made me go on a few years ago."

Janel laughed, trying to ease the tension. "Oh, that ride! Do you remember how you got sick all over the people behind us?"

They both laughed momentarily, and Wilma could almost feel the stress easing, if only a touch. "I suppose that was just preparing me for weeks of hugging the toilet, huh?"

"Listen, Wilma," Janel said, her tone softening. "I've been doing some research. There are things you can do to lessen chemo's effects on your body. Changing your diet and medication, taking it easy. And you don't have to go through it alone. I'm right here if you need me, and I have a hunch Seth would be, too, if you'd let him."

Wilma felt a pang of guilt at the reminder. She bit her lip. "How can you be there for me? You're six hundred miles away."

"That means nothing to me," Janel replied. "I've already requested time off if need be, and I'm not letting you face this alone."

Wilma's throat tightened, her heart swelling with gratitude. "I know you wouldn't, Janel. Thank you... for everything."

Wilma felt some weight lift as they continued talking, knowing she had Janel's unwavering support. With her friend's strength beside her, maybe—just maybe—she'd find the courage to let Seth in too.

Wilma snorted; her laughter laced with sarcasm. "So, we're really making good on that whole 'friends who hold each other's hair back while they puke' promise, huh? You're going to get to see that up close and personal."

"Janel… thank you. What would I do without you?"

Janel's laugh bubbled through the phone, brightening Wilma's spirits. "Oh, please. Without me, you'd lead a way more boring life… and who would keep you in check?"

"Wilma? You're going to tell Seth, right?"

With a dramatic sigh, Wilma replied, "Alright, alright. I'll tell him today. What's the worst he can do? Leave me?" She gave a wry chuckle, but a hint of uncertainty lingered in the air.

Wilma tossed her phone on the coffee table, twisted on the sofa, and peered out the window. Late morning filtered through the windows of Wilma's cozy second-floor apartment. She gazed over the rooftops that stretched across the town. From this vantage point, she could see the scattered chimneys and shingled roofs, an old water tower in the distance, and the quaint patterns of small-town life unfolding below. The familiar sight usually brought her comfort, but today, her thoughts were muddled, drifting to her conversation with Janel and the nerve-wracking conversation she'd soon have with Seth.

She pulled on a sweatshirt and tied her sneakers. Maybe a walk would clear her head. She needed to ground herself, find a moment of peace before the whirlwind of emotions she anticipated later. Grabbing her keys, she sent Seth a quick text message: *Can you stop by later? There's something I need to talk to you about.* She hit "send" before she could second-guess herself, then tucked her phone away and stepped out into the fresh air.

The quiet back road wound between fields and tidy farmhouses, each with its own simple charm that was unmistakably Amish. Wooden fences lined the road, and laundry flapped on clotheslines in the gentle breeze, muted colors blending into the landscape. Wilma inhaled deeply, the scent of freshly turned earth and budding spring blossoms surrounding her, and felt a calm settle over her.

Without realizing it, her steps led her toward Ruth's farm. She was certain that a few moments in Ruth's company, with the simplicity and quiet around them, might help her find the words she needed to share with Seth later.

As she approached the big wrap-around porch of the picture-perfect farmhouse, Wilma paused, feeling the warmth of Ruth's friendship even from afar. This small piece of the Amish world had a way of grounding her, helping her see things through a different, quieter lens.

***

Ruth settled onto the porch swing, patting the seat beside her as Wilma joined her, settling in with a satisfied sigh. They watched in comfortable silence as robins picked at the ground nearby, tugging up worms and darting around with spring's new energy. After a while, Ruth looked over, noting the tension on Wilma's face.

"You look troubled," Ruth said peacefully.

Wilma let out a tired laugh. "Troubled is putting it lightly. It's like my life's going at full speed, and I'm just along for the ride. Treatment starts next week, and my friend convinced me it's time to tell Seth everything... tonight."

Ruth nodded, listening without judgment as Wilma leaned forward, placing her hands under her thighs, almost as if bracing herself. "I guess part of me thinks this is all just a bad dream. That I'll wake up and life will be normal again... whatever normal is."

They sat in silence for a while, letting the sounds of spring speak louder than words, until Ruth asked, "Have you ever been to the ocean?"

Wilma's face lit up, and she swooned a little at the memory. "Ahh, yes! Sanibel Island on Florida's Gulf Coast. It's my happy place. The last few years have been rough on it, though, what with hurricanes and everything. But still, nothing beats the salty air and the beat of the waves hitting the shoreline."

Ruth smiled, drawn in by Wilma's enthusiasm. "I've never

been, but I had plans to visit my aunt in Pinecraft soon. She promised to take me to Siesta Key. They say the ocean there is the prettiest blue."

"It is!" Wilma replied, nearly bouncing in her seat. "The sand's like powder, and the water... it's like nothing you've ever seen. You'd love it."

Ruth's smile softened, a wistful look passing over her face. "It does sound wonderful, but I'm not sure that trip is in my future. Traveling right after surgery... it's a lot. And that's a long bus ride without proper rest."

Wilma stopped the swing with her foot, her expression turning serious. "Then we'll go together. I'll drive us down, and we can take our time, stopping wherever we want along the way."

Ruth's heart skipped at the thought, and for a moment, she felt like a girl again, imagining adventures down long, open roads. But she quickly tempered her excitement. "Oh, Wilma, I couldn't ask that of you."

"Ruth, please. This isn't just for you—it's for both of us. It'll give us something to look forward to, something more than hospitals and recovery. We can plan for the sunshine and the sea, for quiet mornings with sand between our toes and no treatments in sight. It's like... a gift to ourselves for making it through."

Ruth chuckled at Wilma's enthusiasm, surprised by how the idea stirred a spark within her, one she hadn't felt in a long time. "Well... it does sound nice. A proper adventure, I'd say. But I'd need to talk it over with Levi."

Wilma's eyes sparkled with excitement. "Perfect! I've already thought about all the places we could visit. We'd start with a drive through West Virginia, soaking up those green hills and charming little towns. Then we'd head to Williamsburg, Virginia... just imagine strolling through all that colonial history! After that, we could swing by Asheville, North Carolina, with its beautiful Blue Ridge views, maybe even stay in a cozy mountain cabin. And of course, we couldn't miss Charleston, with all the old architecture, and Savannah—oak trees dripping with Spanish moss like something out of a dream."

Ruth laughed, swept up in Wilma's contagious excitement. "My, you've really thought this through fast, haven't you?"

"Oh, I've practically got the whole itinerary already planned," Wilma replied, grinning. "We'll hit every quirky roadside stand and scenic overlook we find. And when we finally reach the ocean, we'll kick off our shoes and feel the sand. After what we have to endure, believe me, that beach will feel like paradise."

Ruth couldn't help but be moved by the vision Wilma was painting, one that seemed almost too good to be true. And yet, the idea of sharing such an adventure, of feeling the ocean's pull for the first time, gave her a sense of peace about the road ahead.

"Well," Ruth said, "it does sound like a bit of heaven on earth. I'll see what Levi thinks." She looked at Wilma, noting the spark of joy in her eyes, and smiled. "But for now, let's just savor the idea. *Gott* willing, we'll make it happen."

***

Wilma fidgeted with the edge of the throw blanket draped over her couch, watching Seth's face as he took in the news she had at last laid out for him. She could see the initial shock, quickly followed by something even harder to bear: sympathy.

He let out a long breath, searching her eyes. "Wilma... this is why you turned down my proposal?"

She crossed her arms, forcing a smirk. "Look, you want a future. Someone who can give you that happy family and house you keep talking about. And here I am, unsure if I'll even have that future."

Seth stooped down in front of her on the couch, his eyes tender, his voice gentle. "Wilma, you're more than enough. I don't need some perfect dream. I want you."

Wilma shook her head, trying to keep her emotions in check. "No, you want a family. And right now, I don't even know if I'll be here in a year, let alone able to have children. I can't bring you into that. It's unfair to you."

His face softened, and he moved to take her hand, but she instantly pulled it back, a defensive edge creeping into her tone. "This isn't something you can fix. I can't promise you anything but a mess. That's what I am right now, and that's what I'll be for a long time, even if things go well."

Seth's jaw tightened, but he remained calm, his voice steady. "Wilma, you don't have to face this alone. I'm here because I *want* to be with you. Not just for the easy times."

She let out a frustrated laugh. "That's easy for you to say now, but this is more than a rough patch. This is surgeries, treatments, and maybe no future beyond that. How can I ask you to give up everything you want—everything you deserve— for something so uncertain?"

Seth stayed silent for a moment, taking in her words. Finally, he said in a soft tone, "I get that you're scared. I'd be lying if I said I wasn't too. But love isn't about guarantees. It's about being there, no matter what comes."

She swallowed; her gaze fixed firmly on the floor. "You deserve someone who can give you more than that. Someone who isn't... broken." Her voice cracked on the last word, but she quickly pulled herself back together.

After a long silence, Seth nodded, clearly hurt but respecting her decision. "Alright, I'll give you space you need, but I'm not giving up on you."

Wilma gave a slight nod, biting back the tears that threatened to spill over. She wasn't ready to let him in—couldn't let him in—until she knew what the future held, however long that might be.

***

Later that afternoon, Ruth wandered over to the bakery to see if Emma needed a hand, knowing Katie was tied up with little Daniel. As she approached the door, the warm, sweet scent of cinnamon rolls and fresh-baked bread filled the air, mingling with the laughter and chatter of a busy afternoon. Inside, every mismatched chair and table was occupied, and a tour group from the local Amish tour company was savoring their mid-afternoon treat.

Ruth took one look at the bustling crowd and knew Emma was in over her head. Without a word, she moved behind the counter and began helping with customers, her hands moving skillfully as she rang up orders, sliced loaves, and filled pastry bags. Emma's tired smile lit up as she caught Ruth's eye, a silent but heartfelt thanks. Within minutes, the line had thinned, and the shop was quiet again, with only a few regulars sitting and enjoying their baked goods.

Emma wiped her brow with the back of her sleeve and checked on the children playing peacefully in a small corner Samuel had built to keep the little ones entertained. She turned to Ruth, her face full of gratitude. "Your timing was perfect! *Denki.*"

Ruth chuckled, patting Emma's arm. "I had a feeling you could use an extra set of hands."

Emma's smile softened, but a hint of concern lingered in her eyes as she glanced at Ruth. She took a deep breath, as if steadying herself, and asked, "Ruth, how are you really? Is there anything we can do to make things easier for you after... well, after the surgery?"

Ruth paused, meeting Emma's worried gaze. She could see the weight of Emma's question, the unspoken pain tied to memories of her own mother's struggle. She placed a comforting hand on Emma's shoulder and said sensitively, "Emma, I know this isn't easy for you. What happened with your *mamm*... I know it's hard to keep that separate from my own journey."

Emma's eyes glistened, and she nodded, swallowing hard. "It's just... hard not to think of it. But I want to be here for you, however I can."

Ruth smiled, her voice calm and reassuring. "Each diagnosis is different, *jah*? Mine isn't like your mother's, and *Gott* has a unique plan for each of us. I've placed my trust in His hands, and by His blood, I am healed, healthy, and well." Ruth's words were firm, her faith unwavering, and Emma seemed to draw comfort from the conviction in her mother-in-law's voice.

Emma's shoulders relaxed, and she managed a small smile. "You're strong. I know you'll face this with courage. But I'm here to help, truly. If there's anything you need, just say the word."

Ruth squeezed her hand, appreciating her daughter-in-law's concern. "Just having you here, ready to lend a hand, is already a blessing. We'll take each day as it comes, one step at a time."

***

Ruth was making a hamloaf for supper when she heard a familiar knock on the door. She looked up to see her friend Susan stepping inside, her expression thoughtful yet a touch more serious than usual.

"*Gut* afternoon, Susan," Ruth greeted with a warm smile. "What brings you by?"

Susan hesitated, folding her hands in front of her. "You know I'm only here out of concern, *jah*?"

Ruth paused, wiping her hands on her apron. "Of course. Come, sit and have some tea."

Susan settled into a chair but didn't touch the tea Ruth poured. Instead, she leaned forward, lowering her voice. "There's talk among some of the women in the community. They're wondering why you're spending so much time with that *Englisch* woman, Wilma Nettles. Some feel that your place is with us; to keep your life and troubles close to those who understand our ways."

Ruth's smile softened, her eyes reflecting kindness and calm. "Wilma may not be one of us, but she's become a friend in a time when she needs it most. *Gott* has a way of bringing people into our lives, and I don't question His purpose in this."

Susan frowned, looking down. "But there's a concern that you're opening up to a stranger, someone who doesn't know our ways or beliefs. Isn't it a risk, sharing so much of yourself with an outsider?"

Ruth met Susan's gaze directly. "If *Gott* has placed Wilma on my path, how can I turn away? She's facing a difficult time, like me." She took a deep breath, her tone steady. "In caring for Wilma, I'm simply following the example our Lord set for us. We are called to love others, no matter who they are or where they come from."

Susan's expression softened, though her brow remained furrowed. "But don't you think it's better to rely on those who understand us? To keep our lives private, especially when facing something as serious as your... situation?"

Ruth took a sip of tea before continuing. "*Jah*, some things might seem different, but I feel a deep peace in my heart about this friendship. We don't always understand why the Lord places certain people on our path, but I trust He has a purpose for every friendship He blesses us with."

Susan sat quietly for a moment. "I suppose... if *Gott* has placed Wilma in your life, there must be a reason."

Ruth gave a stern nod. "Please, let the others know they have nothing to worry about. My heart is in the community, as it always has been. But if I can bring a little of our love and faith to Wilma, I will gladly do so, regardless of what others might think." Ruth took a deep breath and added, "At the end of my days, I'll stand before *Gott* alone."

Ruth watched as Susan's shoulders slumped at her statement. She didn't mean to upset her old friend, but she was certain that the good Lord had placed the young *Englisch* woman in her care for a reason, and she wasn't about to tell Him no.

CHAPTER 7

Ruth stood under the hot spray, feeling the warmth cascade over her shoulders, grounding her as she prepared for what lay ahead. The steam wrapped around her, a fleeting comfort in the stillness of the morning. Her heart felt heavy with the gravity of the day, yet her mind drifted to a place of quiet trust, a refuge she had clung to more than ever in these past weeks.

The past three weeks had been a test of her faith, a call to rely on the Lord's strength over her own understanding. Each day, she had pushed aside her doubts, choosing instead to lean into the promises she held dear. *The Lord had walked before her, knowing the path and preparing the way.* It was a thought she repeated over and over, a reminder that her strength was not her own but a gift from *Gott*.

With trembling hands, she traced over the parts of herself that would soon be changed, allowing herself to feel the loss but not to dwell there. Instead, she whispered a prayer, her voice barely audible over the steady stream of water. *"Lord, Your will is my strength. I will trust You, even when the path is unknown. I lean not on my understanding but on Yours."*

A calm washed over her heart as she fell to her knees, feeling the closeness of her Creator in that small, private space. The weight lifted, replaced by a quiet certainty that she could face the day ahead, not because she was strong, but because her strength was rooted in the One who had promised never to forsake her.

She rose slowly, drying off and wrapping herself in a robe as a gentle knock came at the door.

"Ruth," Levi called out, "are you almost ready? Samuel and Emma are here with the driver. We'll need to leave in a few minutes."

Ruth drew in a steady breath, finding peace in the promise she clung to. "*Jah,*" she replied, her voice softened by the prayer that now filled her heart. "I'll be right out. My bag's by the front door."

As she looked at her reflection, Ruth saw someone different—a woman stepping forward not in her own strength, but in the faith that had carried her through every trial. The road ahead remained uncertain, but her heart held onto one truth: *By His blood, I am healed.* With that promise, she stepped from the room, ready to walk the path laid before her with the unshakeable assurance that she was never alone.

Suddenly, Wilma came to mind, and Ruth prayed that her friend would feel a peace so deep today that she could only attribute it to the Lord's presence.

***

A fresh wave of tears rolled down Wilma's cheeks, landing on her bare shoulders as she looked away from her reflection. Her face, usually composed, was blotched and unfamiliar, the fear all too real and visible. She turned from the mirror, forcing herself into a robotic routine, brushing her teeth, fixing her hair, moving as if on autopilot. She pushed her emotions aside, trying to keep herself from falling into a spiral she feared she couldn't pull herself out of.

In the quiet of the bathroom, she thought of Ruth, her steadfast strength in the face of the same trial. Ruth seemed to have a wellspring of peace, some unseen force she leaned on as naturally as she breathed. And here she was, drowning in a mixture of fear and doubt, clinging only to her own strength.

A sudden, unexplainable calm washed over her, just enough to steady her trembling hands. Her mind drifted back to the conversations she'd had with Ruth, to the quiet way Ruth had spoken about faith and leaning into something greater than herself. Wilma took a shaky breath, feeling an ache rise in her chest—a strange longing for the peace that seemed to come so easily to Ruth.

But *how*? How could she even begin to find that kind of faith? She didn't know where to start, or if she was even capable of trusting in something she couldn't see. Yet in that moment, there was a sense of calm so unfamiliar it almost frightened her. She clutched it tightly, her heart whispering words she didn't fully understand, hoping that maybe, somehow, she could begin to grasp the faith Ruth had shown her.

***

Ruth sat quietly on the edge of the hospital bed, her legs swinging casually as she waited for the nurse to finish setting up. She wrapped the thin blanket around her lap, rubbing her arms against the chill in the sterile room. A strange calm settled over her, one she knew wasn't of her own making. She whispered a prayer of thanks, feeling the quiet presence of the Lord holding her steady.

Moments later, Levi peeked his head around the door, his gaze soft but clearly searching her face. He was followed closely by Samuel and Emma, their expressions a mixture of worry and love. "The nurse said we could stay with you until they came to take you for surgery," Levi murmured, stepping fully into the room and taking her hand.

Ruth's face lit up with a grateful smile. Seeing them there warmed her, even as she took note of the concern etched on each of their faces. "Please," she said gently, "there's no need to worry."

Levi sat beside her, patting the back of her hand tenderly. "It's hard not to be concerned, Ruth. Seeing you here... well, it just doesn't feel right."

She looked down at their hands clasped together and gave him a tiny squeeze before looking up at Emma and Samuel, who hovered nearby with uncertainty in their eyes. "I know. But remember, this is not a surprise to *Gott*. Every step of this journey has been known to Him, even when it seems unknown to us."

Emma took a shaky breath, her eyes glistening. "It's hard to see it that way, *Mamm*. But your faith... it amazes me."

Ruth's smile softened, her voice calm but unwavering. "I have faith, *jah,* and I'm holding onto it tightly. No matter what happens, He will be glorified through this. We might not see it today, or even next week, but He will be glorified. That is a certainty I carry with me into this day."

Samuel and Emma exchanged a glance, visibly moved, while Levi sat by her side, seeming to draw strength from her words. Ruth closed her eyes briefly, sending a silent prayer of gratitude for the family who surrounded her, trusting that they, too, would find comfort in the One who held all things in His hands.

When she opened her eyes again, she saw a hint of peace settle over them, a shared understanding that whatever lay ahead, they would walk it together, held by a faith that couldn't be shaken.

***

Janel, ever the loyal friend, had driven all the way from South Carolina to be by Wilma's side for her first treatment.

She offered Wilma a gentle smile, the kind that needed no words. In that quiet moment, they let their lifelong friendship speak for them, filling the silence with a shared understanding and support that only years of companionship could bring.

As Janel maneuvered the car through the crowded parking lot, Wilma glanced down at her phone, the screen lighting up with a string of texts from Seth. She could see his frustration woven between the words, a reminder of how hurt he felt about her decision to go alone to her first chemotherapy treatment.

She loved him, truly, she did, but letting him get so deeply entangled in her health struggles didn't feel right. There was a line between support and entanglement, and she couldn't bear the thought of him watching her grow weaker. She hurriedly typed a promise to text him when her appointment was over, then tucked her phone into her bag, fighting the emptiness his absence left in her heart.

As she stepped into the oncology center, Wilma felt her pulse quicken. She laid her hand on the small, raised area of her chest where they'd inserted a port just a week before, a constant reminder of the battle her body was about to undergo. Taking a deep breath, she forced herself forward, following the quiet hum of voices and the beeps of monitors.

The treatment room was quiet yet bustling, a strange combination of calm and clinical. Reclining chairs lined the walls, each paired with an IV pole and a small table littered with books, magazines, and half-finished water bottles. She could see nurses moving quietly from patient to patient, checking IVs and adjusting lines with soft voices and careful touches.

As she settled into her own chair by the window, she glanced around the room, taking in the faces around her… some weary, some hopeful, but all with a shared, unspoken understanding. A nurse approached her, holding a clear IV line, and smiled kindly. "Are you ready, Wilma?" she asked, her voice gentle.

Wilma nodded, though her heart raced, and her stomach twisted with a mixture of dread and determination. The nurse explained the process, her words distant as Wilma focused on the clear tubing, the sterile scent of antiseptic, and the steady hum of the machines. She flinched considerably as the nurse connected the line to her port, feeling each slow, deliberate drip, a stark reminder of the reality she was now living.

She closed her eyes, trying to block out the unfamiliar sounds… the soft murmurs, the beeps, the faint hum of the overhead lights. She wanted to be anywhere but here, somewhere far from the sterile walls and fluorescent lights.

Yet beneath the fear and uncertainty, a strange presence lingered, something she couldn't quite explain. Her thoughts drifted to Ruth. *How did she find it?* Wilma wondered. *How could anyone feel peace in a place like this?*

The nurse placed a comforting hand on her shoulder, bringing her back to the present. Wilma managed a weak smile, determined to find her own way through the fear, even if she wasn't sure where to start.

***

Time seemed to slow as Ruth was wheeled through the long hallway toward the pre-surgical floor, each passing moment stretching out in silence. She watched the ceiling lights blur above her, the low hum of machinery and distant footsteps filling the space around her. When they reached the pre-op area, the nurse guided her bed into a line of other patients' cubicles, each waiting their turn for surgery. With a gentle pat on her foot, the nurse offered a soft smile before stepping away, leaving Ruth alone in the quiet.

The sounds of the room… occasional beeps, soft murmurs,

the distant whirr of equipment seemed to press in on her, unfamiliar and almost gloomy. Her heart quickened, a surge of fear welling up that she couldn't quite push aside. She closed her eyes, whispering a prayer, *Lord, calm my heart. Surround me with Your peace.*

Focusing on the soft glow of the overhead lights, she took a deep breath, finding strength in the rhythm of her own breathing. Then, like a whisper on the edge of her thoughts, a clear message filled her heart: *I've sent My angels before you.*

An unexplainable calm settled over her, spreading warmth through her entire body. She felt the weight of her fear lift, replaced by a gentle peace she knew could only come from *Gott*. Just then, the anesthesiologist approached, introducing himself with a reassuring nod as he added something to her IV. The nurse wheeled her swiftly toward the operating room, her words kind and comforting, though Ruth hardly registered them. She was focused inward, holding onto the calm *Gott* had given her.

Once inside the sterile, cold room, she shivered as she was helped onto the surgical table, the chill of the metal beneath her a stark reminder of the road ahead. She closed her eyes, the bright lights above nearly blinding, and whispered her breath prayer, the words forming a quiet shield around her heart. *You are my God. You are with me. I will trust You in all things.*

As she drifted to sleep, she felt wrapped in a presence far beyond her own understanding—a peace that held her securely, knowing she was carried forward in the Lord's hands.

***

Later that evening, Ruth drifted in and out of sleep, her mind foggy but vaguely aware of Levi's steady presence beside her bed. The room was dim, except for the bed light overhead and the quiet hum of machines nearby. She turned her head, catching sight of Levi with his pocket Bible open on his lap, his head bowed as he mouthed familiar words.

"Psalm 91?" she whispered, her voice barely more than a murmur.

He looked up, a soft smile on his face, and nodded silently.

"Read it to me," she requested, her eyes heavy but hopeful.

Levi cleared his throat gradually and began, his voice steady and soothing as he read aloud the words of the Psalm, each line like a comfort to her spirit. Ruth closed her eyes, letting the familiar verses wash over her, bringing a deep sense of comfort and assurance that wrapped around her like a warm blanket.

When he finished, she reached for his hand, instinctively squeezing it, though the motion sent a slight twinge through her chest beneath the weight of the pressure blankets. She flinched slightly but tried to keep her face composed. Levi noticed and slid his chair closer, bringing her hand to his lips before kissing her forehead lightly.

"How are you doing, *mei lieb*?" he asked in a hushed tone, concern etched in his eyes.

"*Gut,*" she mouthed, giving him a faint smile.

Levi brushed a strand of hair from her face, his gaze soft and reassuring. "The surgeon was in while you were asleep. He said your surgery was... 'boring,'" he added with a smirk. "Which, in his words, is exactly how he hopes all his surgeries go. He'll be back in the morning to check on you."

Ruth chuckled delicately, she breathed the words, her tone fragile and muted. "Boring? I don't think anyone's ever called me that before."

Levi laughed, his eyes crinkling with warmth. "*Nee*, not one word I'd ever use to describe you." He paused, resting a hand on hers. "Samuel and Emma went home to the *kinner*, and Katie called. I let her know you were resting and promised to leave a message in the phone shanty first thing in the morning."

Ruth's thoughts drifted back to her moment on the operating table, the calm that had washed over her, and the distinct feeling that angels had surrounded her. She wanted to share that experience with Levi, but something held her back, as if the memory was a sacred gift meant only for her heart. For now, she'd keep that precious moment close, letting it be a quiet source of strength through the coming days of recovery.

CHAPTER 8

Wilma held the phone away from her ear, wincing as Seth's frustration finally boiled over. "I don't care that you've lost your hair! When are you going to understand that I love you, and all I want is to support you through this?"

She could hear the defeated sigh on the other end, and her heart clenched. She hated how much she was hurting him by keeping him at a distance. He softened, his voice pleading, "It's been almost two months, I just want to see you. Nothing more, nothing less. No commitments, no promises—just let me see you, please."

Tears welled up in her eyes as his words chipped away at the wall she had carefully built around her heart. "Seth, it's… it's not pretty. I can barely stand to look at myself in the mirror. How am I supposed to let you see me like this?"

"How many times do I have to say it? I don't care about that," he replied, his tone earnest. "Please, just let me be there for you."

She finally conceded, exhausted and unable to resist his heartfelt plea any longer. "Fine… I'll be home tonight."

Trying to lighten the mood and give herself a shred of normalcy, she added with a small smile, "And I expect a double-crust pizza in your hands when you walk through that door."

His relieved laugh brought a flicker of warmth to her heart, and for the first time in weeks, she felt a hint of anticipation. After she hung up, she took a deep breath and glanced around her apartment. The last two months had taken a toll on her space—and on her spirit. Determined to regain a little control, she pushed herself off the couch and began tidying up, picking up clutter and dusting off surfaces. She was ready to reclaim a small piece of herself, and today was the day to start.

After a quick look around to ensure everything was in place, she felt a renewed sense of purpose. Her mind turned to Ruth, whose calm and faith had been her anchor through many difficult days. Deciding she needed her friend's quiet wisdom before facing Seth, she grabbed her keys, pulled on a cheerful hat that hid her bare head, and set off for Ruth's farm.

***

Ruth sat on the swing, gently rocking back and forth as she balanced two-month-old Daniel Jr. on her shoulder. She adjusted the baby carefully, mindful of her tender spots, and nestled her nose into the soft crook of his neck, breathing in his sweet, powdery scent. The simple act filled her with joy, a precious reminder of life's goodness. Today was the first time Katie had left him in her care since returning to work at the bakery, and Ruth relished every second of it.

Life on the Yoder farm was beginning to regain its familiar rhythm. That morning, she'd spent a few peaceful moments in her flower garden, pulling up small weeds and collecting peas from the vegetable bed.

After weeks of resting and relying on others, it felt good to return to her daily routines, grounding her in the life she loved. Though she was still recovering from her surgery, her strength was returning. She'd taken up a new regimen, taking long walks around the farm each day and cutting out the sugary treats she once enjoyed. These small changes, alongside the Lord's grace, had propelled her health to a new level.

Cradling little Daniel Jr. closer, Ruth closed her eyes briefly and whispered a prayer. "Thank You, Lord, for walking with me, for every step You guided me through this journey. I'm grateful for the peace You brought to my heart and for the healing I feel in my body." A gentle warmth spread through her, and she felt her spirit lighten, the worries of the past months easing in the presence of *Gott's* faithfulness.

Ruth opened her eyes at the familiar crunch of gravel under tires, glancing up to see Wilma's car rolling up the driveway. The bright pink of Wilma's hat caught the sunlight as she stepped out, creating a cheerful pop of color against the earthy tones of the farm. Wilma made her way up to the porch, her smile wide and warm, bringing a sense of energy that lifted Ruth's spirits even more.

Ruth looked up as Wilma approached, her face glowing with excitement, framed by the bright pink hat perched playfully on her head. She smiled as she settled into the seat next to Ruth, the usual seriousness of her treatment journey momentarily replaced with a spark of anticipation.

"I have some news," Wilma began, her voice tinged with excitement. "I'm at a break in my chemotherapy. It'll be about a month before my surgery, so I thought… what better time to take that road trip to Pinecraft we talked about?"

Ruth's eyebrows lifted, a bit of surprise mingling with her own excitement. "So soon? Are you sure it's a good time?"

"Oh, it's the perfect time," Wilma reassured her, her eyes bright with eagerness. "Imagine it—a few weeks break from hospitals, needles, and all the medical routine. We'll drive at our own pace, stopping to see everything along the way. I need this, Ruth. I think… maybe we both do."

Ruth couldn't help but feel her own apprehension, wondering if the journey might be too much, but as she looked at Wilma, she saw a joy she hadn't seen in her friend's face for a long time. "When would you like to leave?"

"The day after tomorrow?"

"*Ach.* I'll need to discuss things with Levi and make sure the girls can handle things here for a few weeks," Ruth replied thoughtfully. "And I should get word to my aunt to let her know we're coming…"

"Don't let it overwhelm you, Ruth. This trip is supposed to be about rest and relaxation. But I admit, the sooner we can leave, the better."

Just then, little Daniel Jr. let out a small wiggle and a soft coo from Ruth's arms. Wilma's expression softened as she looked down at the baby. "Can I hold him?"

"Of course," Ruth replied, carefully transferring the tiny bundle into Wilma's arms. Daniel snuggled against her chest and drifted back into sleep, his soft breaths a soothing rhythm.

For a few minutes, Ruth watched as Wilma held Daniel close, her face a mixture of tenderness and longing. But then, as if a sudden thought had struck her, Wilma's expression changed. Her gaze grew distant, her eyes clouded as a shadow of sorrow crossed her face. Almost too quickly, she handed Daniel back to Ruth, her hands trembling a bit.

Ruth sensed the weight of something unspoken in the gesture. "Are you alright?"

Wilma swallowed hard, looking away to hide the tears brimming in her eyes. "I… it's nothing," she replied, though the emotion in her voice betrayed her. "It's just… holding him made me wonder if I'll ever…"

Ruth reached out, resting a comforting hand on Wilma's arm. "The Lord's plans for us aren't always what we expect, but He knows our hearts."

As soon as she handed Daniel back to Ruth, Wilma seemed to shrug off the heaviness that had clouded her eyes moments before. With her usual spark, she launched into the details of their road trip, ticking off each potential stop with a playful glint in her eye. "And we absolutely have to go to Charleston—do you know how many ridiculous souvenirs we can find there? You can't say you've traveled if you don't come back with something completely impractical."

Ruth chuckled, shaking her head at Wilma's playful antics. She'd come to appreciate the girl's bold and forthright manner, especially in these more difficult moments. It was Wilma's way of keeping her spirit afloat, like a lifeline woven from humor and wit.

"Oh, and I made plans to see Seth tonight," Wilma added offhandedly, as if it were an afterthought.

Ruth tilted her head, catching the subtle shift in Wilma's tone. "How do you feel about letting Seth back into your life?"

Wilma let out an exaggerated sigh, folding her arms as if preparing for a battle. "Honestly? It terrifies me. He's like this big, sappy romantic who actually wants to be there for me. Can you imagine?" She rolled her eyes in mock exasperation, then softened, her humor giving way to a quieter confession. "But… I do miss him. I miss the normal things—the silly dates, the late-night talks. But when I think about the future…" She paused, biting her lip. "It's hard to see anything clearly past the surgery. It's like someone's drawn a big foggy line over everything that used to make sense."

Ruth nodded, understanding the deep uncertainties weighing on Wilma's heart. "It's natural to feel that way," she said. "When things are uncertain, *Gott* often places people in our lives to help us through these times. And you know, Seth might just be one of those people."

Wilma gave a small, wry smile, her eyes glinting with her familiar mischief. "So you're saying I should let him tag along for this rollercoaster, huh? It'll be like a twisted version of those romantic comedies. Only instead of sweeping me off my feet, he'll be helping me shuffle to the bathroom with my IV pole." She chuckled, though there was a hint of vulnerability beneath her words.

Ruth laughed, shaking her head, but her expression was tender. "Sometimes letting someone in isn't about knowing the end of the story. It's about allowing someone to be there with you, trusting that together, you'll find a way forward, whatever that may look like."

Wilma took in Ruth's words, letting them settle over her. "Yeah," she murmured, looking down at her hands. "I guess maybe he deserves that choice… even if he might get stuck with a half-bald, snack-obsessed, sarcastic chemo patient for a girlfriend." She smirked, her humor slipping back into place as a shield.

Ruth smiled and said, "Well, I'd say he's lucky to have her."

***

Wilma took a final look at herself in the mirror, adjusting the brightly colored scarf on her head. The bold blues and purples lifted her spirits, but she still felt a pang of nervousness. This was the first time she was letting Seth see her like this, after all these weeks of shutting him out. With a shaky breath, she opened the door.

Seth stood there, a large pizza box in one hand and a small bouquet of flowers in the other. His face softened the moment he saw her, his usual ease clouded by something deeper.

"Pizza and flowers?" she joked, trying to cover her discomfort with sarcasm. "Didn't know you'd be trying to charm a chemo patient with double crust and daisies."

But Seth's smile was tight, his eyes searching her face. He walked in slowly, setting the pizza and flowers on the table without a word. He finally looked at her directly, his voice low and steady. "Wilma… I just want to know why."

She faltered, not expecting the question. "Why, what?"

"Why you shut me out for two months. Why you wouldn't let me help or even see you." His words were calm, but she could hear the hurt behind them. "I mean, you left me completely in the dark, and I had no idea how you were doing. You wouldn't even let me in the door."

Wilma opened her mouth to respond, but the words stuck in her throat. After a few seconds, she sighed, running her hands over her scarf. "I didn't want you to see me like this," she admitted, her tone clipped, a defense mechanism. "I wanted to handle it on my own."

"So that's what you think I am?" Seth shot back, his voice rising just slightly. "Someone to keep out when things get hard? Just someone for pizza and small talk?"

She flinched, his words hitting a nerve. "It's not like that," she said, her voice shaking with both anger and vulnerability. "I needed space, Seth. This—" she motioned to herself "—isn't exactly the picture-perfect version of me, alright? I can't expect you to deal with that."

Seth's gaze softened, his frustration giving way to something deeper. "Wilma, I don't care about the 'picture-perfect' version of you. I want *you,* however you come." He took a step closer, his voice gentler but firm. "And just so you know, I'm not going anywhere."

She swallowed, the urge to push him away battling with a desire to let him in. "I don't need you to be my caregiver," she muttered, her tone softening but still guarded. "I don't want you to rearrange your life because of me."

"But that's my choice," he said simply. "Let me make it."

She took a deep breath, her eyes dropping to the floor. "I'm going to Florida. I'm taking a trip with Ruth. I need a break—a real one—before my surgery." She looked up at him, bracing for his reaction.

Seth's face shifted, a mix of surprise and concern. "You're going to Florida? Now?"

"Yes," she replied, lifting her chin defiantly. "I need this. I need to feel like *me* again, not just someone counting down doctor appointments and surgeries. And I don't need anyone's permission to live my life, not even yours."

Seth let out a frustrated sigh, his hands clenched at his sides. "You're right. You don't need my permission. But is it so wrong for me to be worried? You're taking this trip while you're still recovering. Can't you see why that scares me?"

Wilma's gaze softened, a hint of vulnerability slipping

through. "I do see, but… I can't let this thing control every part of me. I need to prove to myself that there's still life outside all this."

They stood in silence for a long moment, the tension heavy but somehow softened by the mutual understanding in their eyes.

Seth reached out, taking her hand. "Then go. Take the trip and find that freedom. But promise me one thing."
She raised an eyebrow. "What?"

"Let me be here when you get back."

She smiled, a small but genuine smile, finally feeling the wall between them start to crack. "Deal. But don't think this means I'm going easy on you. I still refuse to make any promises that I might be unable to keep."

Seth laughed, pulling her into a gentle hug. "I'd expect nothing less."

***

Early the next morning, Ruth poured Levi a fresh cup of coffee and set his breakfast before him. The quiet kitchen filled with soft light as the sun climbed over the horizon, peeking in through the window. Outside, the familiar scent of strawberries drifted in through the open window, mingling with the aroma of breakfast.

Levi took a sip, glancing over at Ruth with a trace of concern. "Are you sure you're up for a trip like this?" he asked, his voice gentle but clearly a little worried.

Ruth met his gaze, a reassuring smile on her face. "I'm certain, Levi. I feel better than I have in years. The changes I've made have given me a new kind of energy." She reached out to rest her hand on his, her expression both steady and warm. "I know it seems like a lot to you, but I feel that *Gott* has something planned for me on this trip."

Levi looked at her with interest, his concern slowly giving way to curiosity. "What do you mean?"

Ruth paused, gathering her thoughts as she looked out the window, watching the morning light dance over the strawberry fields. "I can't explain it exactly, but I feel… called to be there for Wilma. Like there's something He wants me to do for her or teach her during this time. I don't know why, but it feels like I'm meant to go on this journey with her."

Levi's brow furrowed considerably, and he nodded, listening intently. "You feel that strongly about it?"

Ruth smiled, a peaceful certainty in her eyes. "*Jah*. I believe *Gott* has already prepared me, brought me through the surgery, and restored my health for a purpose. And I have this sense that my being with Wilma is part of that purpose."

Levi gave her hand a gentle squeeze, a look of admiration crossing his face. "I've always known you to be strong, but this is something else, Ruth. It's as though your faith has only deepened through all this."

Ruth nodded. "It has. I've come to understand that my life is truly in His hands. By His grace, I don't need to hold on to fear about my health or the future. I just trust Him, knowing He'll guide me on the path He has planned." She paused, giving Levi a gentle smile. "I'll take good care of myself on this trip, and I'll come home with more stories than you'll know what to do with."

Levi chuckled. "Alright, alright, I get it. You're going on this adventure, and I wouldn't dare stop you."

She leaned over, planting a gentle kiss on his cheek. "I promise I'll take it easy. And thank you for letting me follow where *Gott* leads, even if it takes me a little farther from home than usual."

With a final squeeze of her hand, Levi nodded, his face both loving and proud. "Then go. Go and do what He has called you to do."

CHAPTER 9

Wilma glanced at Ruth as they made their way down the driveway, her eyes sparkling with anticipation. "Ready for our big adventure?" she asked, gripping the steering wheel with excitement.

Ruth smiled, waving to Levi as he stood at the edge of the driveway, watching them pull away. She gave a little wave, her face softening. "I can't believe this is really happening," she murmured, resting a hand on her stomach as if to steady the fluttering butterflies within. "It's strange, leaving home. I've never been away from Levi and the *kinner* this long."

"Well, get used to it. This is your chance to relax and just be you," Wilma said, turning on the radio and scrolling through stations. She stopped when she landed on a soft folk tune. "You alright with a little music?"

Ruth's eyebrows lifted in surprise. "I don't know what I'd like, to be honest! We don't listen to music."

Wilma laughed and moved to turn it off, but Ruth shook her head, resting a gentle hand on Wilma's. "No, keep it. I wouldn't mind hearing what you enjoy. This trip is about exploring and new experiences, *jah*?"

Wilma grinned. "Well then, how adventurous are you feeling? I could give you a tour of all kinds of music—country, gospel, bluegrass… or maybe a little jazz?" she teased.

Ruth gave a light chuckle, straightening out a fold in her dress. "Oh my, I wouldn't know where to start. Maybe something a bit slower?"

"Deal. I'll keep us on the mellow side," Wilma said, easing the car onto the open road. "This is your vacation, too, so don't hesitate to speak up. It's about what we both want, and I'm not here to pressure you into anything that doesn't feel right."

Ruth smiled, glancing out the window as the familiar Pennsylvania countryside began to blur by. "I'll trust you to guide me in this. Just don't be surprised if I need a few moments to adjust."

They drove in comfortable silence for a while, the gentle strum of acoustic guitars playing faintly from the speakers as the rolling hills of Pennsylvania began to fade behind them. Ruth relaxed, letting herself settle into the moment, the nerves in her stomach slowly giving way to a sense of calm.

As the miles ticked by, she realized she'd never had a chance quite like this—a moment of freedom, of exploring new places with a friend, all while trusting that *Gott* had a purpose in every step.

*****

Ruth's fingers gripped the door handle as Wilma navigated her way through Pittsburgh's bustling traffic on Interstate 79. The towering buildings, the crisscrossing bridges, and the endless lines of cars were a far cry from the peaceful Amish countryside Ruth was used to. Her eyes darted from side to side, catching sight of the roaring vehicles surrounding them as Wilma skillfully switched lanes.

"Are you doing alright?" Wilma asked, a teasing smile tugging at her lips as she noticed Ruth's tight grip.

Ruth forced a small laugh. "*Jah*, just not quite used to this… speed."

Wilma grinned. "Welcome to the Englisher side of the world," she replied, gently pressing on the gas as they continued south. Just as they crossed into West Virginia, a sign appeared for a rest stop, and Wilma pulled off the highway, eager to stretch their legs.

The rest area was peaceful, a mix of shady trees and picnic benches set against the backdrop of rolling hills. As they walked along the sidewalk, Ruth took in the fresh air, visibly relaxing now that they were away from the fast-paced highway.

As they headed back to the car, a young woman, holding her daughter's hand walked toward them, her gaze landing on Wilma's bright scarf. She paused, giving a warm smile, and then approached them.

"Hi, I don't mean to intrude, but I just felt led to ask… would it be alright if I prayed for you?" she asked, her eyes reflecting kindness as she looked at Wilma.

Caught off guard, Wilma blinked, exchanging a look with Ruth before responding. "Um… sure, I suppose," she replied, feeling a bit self-conscious yet touched by the woman's sincerity.

The woman bowed her head, murmuring a simple prayer for strength, health, and peace. Wilma stood still, unsure of how to respond but oddly comforted by the gesture. When the woman finished, she offered a quick smile and continued on her way with her daughter.

Back in the car, Wilma shook her head, glancing at Ruth with a bewildered expression. "That was… weird. Do people often just stop and pray for strangers like that?"

Ruth chuckled. "I've always believed that when the Lord moves someone to pray for another, there's a reason behind it. He places a gentle nudge in our hearts, and if we're listening, we respond."

Wilma took in Ruth's words, mulling them over. "I guess I'm just not used to it. Felt strange to have someone stop their day just to say a prayer for me."

"Think of it this way," Ruth said, her voice warm and steady. "Accepting someone's prayer is like receiving a blessing. When we open ourselves to it, we're allowing the Lord to work through others. You didn't take away her time— you gave her the chance to share *Gott's* love with you."

Wilma nodded thoughtfully, feeling a bit of the tension ease from her shoulders as they got back on the road.

As Ruth settled back into her seat, she glanced over at Wilma. "Where are we stopping for the night?"

Wilma smiled, her face softening with the memory. "We're staying with my mom's closest friends, Sandy and Ted. They practically helped raise me. They live in West Virginia, and they're the closest thing I have to family. They invited us to stay for the night before we continued on our journey."

Ruth smiled, sensing how this visit might be good for Wilma. "I'm looking forward to meeting them."

***

Both women fell into a comfortable silence as the car wove through the twisting, narrow roads leading along Tenmile Creek, West Virginia. The highway had rapidly transformed into a scenic route, with dense green forests pressing in on both sides.

Early June had painted the mountains deep green, speckled with wildflowers in bursts of purple and yellow, and the occasional deer darted into view before disappearing as hastily as it appeared.

"Isn't it beautiful?" Wilma asked, breaking the silence. She gestured toward a small stream trickling down the hillside and merging into Tenmile Creek, which had grown more visible as they neared their destination.

"*Jah*, it's something else," Ruth murmured, her eyes following the stream.

By the time they pulled up to Sandy and Ted's home, a modest house perched on a small hill overlooking the creek, the sun was dipping in the late afternoon sky. Sandy and Ted were already outside, waving from the porch with welcoming smiles. Wilma's heart lifted. Being here brought a comforting familiarity.

After warm embraces, they settled onto the back porch with glasses of sweet tea. The back porch stretched wide, opening up to an unobstructed view of Tenmile Creek winding through the valley. Ruth, taking in the calm setting, seemed right at home despite being miles from Pennsylvania.

Sandy began to reminisce, telling stories about Wilma's mother, Margaret, and their shared childhood. Ted chimed in with tales of their adventures in the mountains, painting a picture of a simpler, joyful time.

Wilma found herself laughing at stories she'd never heard before, feeling the warmth of shared memories fill the spaces left by her mother's absence.

After a while, Wilma excused herself to walk down to the creek with Ted, who wanted to show her some of the places where her mother and Sandy had played as children. As she walked away, she cast a glance back at Ruth and Sandy, sitting side by side on the porch swing.

Sandy turned to Ruth, her voice softening with concern. "I wish I could do more to help the girl. She's putting on a brave face, but I know she's carrying more than she lets on."

Ruth nodded, a look of understanding in her eyes. "Wilma's strong, but even the strongest need a shoulder to lean on."

Sandy sighed, her gaze resting on the creek below. "I know she has faith somewhere deep down, but she's been lost since her mother passed. I'm hoping this trip with you will help her find it again."

Ruth gave a gentle smile. "I pray so."

They sipped their tea in silence, both women united in their hope for Wilma's healing—of the heart as much as her body. As dusk settled over the valley, they watched Wilma and Ted make their way back up the path, laughing and talking as though the weight of the last few months had lightened, if only for a moment.

***

After an early breakfast, Wilma and Ruth joined Sandy and Ted on the gravel road leading to the small country church nestled within the trees. The church stood humbly against the green backdrop, a simple white building with a wooden cross worn by years of West Virginia weather.

As they stepped through the doors, Wilma's eyes were drawn to the stained-glass window above the pulpit, where light filtered through onto the worn pews. She hadn't stepped into a church since her mother's passing, and a pang of doubt hit her. How could she turn to God now when He hadn't been there in her mother's darkest hour?

Meanwhile, Ruth took in the sanctuary's simplicity, observing the congregation's warmth. People greeted one another with embraces and open smiles, and it felt different from the orderly greetings and reserved nature of her church at home. Ruth respected the openness but felt drawn to her own way of worship, structured and quiet, where trust in *Gott* was often unspoken yet deeply felt.

The service began, and the congregation opened their hymnals, filling the room with song. Ruth's eyes softened as she recognized the tune, and she sang with her usual quiet intensity, her voice blending with Sandy's in a harmonious embrace of *Gott's* glory.

When the pastor's message touched on faith amid

uncertainty, Wilma felt herself tense up, memories of her mother's last days rising unbidden in her mind. Her doubts deepened as she listened, wondering how anyone could still believe when faced with such loss. But she couldn't deny the flicker of peace that washed over her; it was faint, yet enough to momentarily quiet her restless heart.

As they returned up the road after the service, Wilma released a sigh, breaking the comfortable silence. "Well, that was... different. Felt like everyone there was reading each other's diaries."

Sandy chuckled, nudging her lightly. "Maybe that's what community is... sharing life's burdens."

"Or oversharing." Wilma grinned, a hint of sarcasm in her voice to mask her discomfort.

Sandy shook her head, smiling knowingly. "You say that, but I think you felt something today inside that church."

Wilma softened, but only briefly before shaking her head with a laugh. "Peace, confusion... who can really tell? I'm not about to figure out life's big questions over a sermon and a hymn or two. But I'll admit, it was... refreshing."

***

Later that day and back on the road, the afternoon sun beat in the car window as Wilma suddenly veered off the road, pulling into the crowded parking lot of a sprawling roadside flea market. The sight left Ruth wide-eyed as she took in the colorful tents and makeshift stalls, bustling with people from all walks of life.

Ruth murmured with an edge of hesitation in her voice. "What are we doing here?"

Wilma grinned, unbuckling her seatbelt with enthusiasm. "Time to introduce you to some more of the world, Ruth. Let's see what kind of treasures we can dig up. Maybe I can find a few silly hats to cover my head. Something that'll make folks take a second look even more."

Ruth returned a soft smile, following Wilma into the maze of tables. They strolled through the flea market, surrounded by a colorful sea of vendors selling everything from handcrafted quilts to rusty farm tools. Ruth kept her arms clasped tightly in front of her, looking cautiously over at Wilma, who was already thumbing through racks of vibrant scarves and beaded necklaces.

As they meandered to another stall, Wilma spotted a bright pink feather boa hanging among an assortment of odd hats. She wrapped it around her neck and struck a dramatic pose, laughing as Ruth's cheeks turned pink. "Come on, live a little!" Wilma teased, giving the boa a little shake.

Ruth managed a small smile, glancing around to see if anyone from home might have somehow wandered into this very non-Amish place. Ultimately, after a long pause, she picked up a simple straw hat and tried it on, adjusting it just so. "This one's… modest," she offered, looking to Wilma for approval.

"It's perfect for you," Wilma said, nodding approvingly. "Just enough style to keep you trendy but still proper."

As they continued, Ruth watched Wilma find joy in every little trinket, and the carefree attitude started to rub off on her. She realized that being here didn't mean she had to compromise her values—it was simply an experience she was sharing with a friend. And maybe, just maybe, this was part of the purpose she felt called toward: showing love and support in the little moments, even if they were unexpected.

Before they left, Ruth found herself holding a dainty porcelain cup with hand-painted roses, something beautiful and understated.

Wilma noticed and leaned over, then whispered. "That old

thing caught your eye, huh?"

Ruth nodded, running her finger nimbly over the delicate handle. "Sometimes, even things that seem worn out still have beauty… and purpose. Perhaps they're just waiting for someone to see them as whole."

Wilma looked at her, a slight smile playing on her lips as she relied. "Are you trying to remind me I'm not as broken as I feel?"

Ruth's gentle, loving eyes met Wilma's. "You're not broken, and you don't need to be perfect to be worth something."

Ruth ran her finger along the rim of the teacup again, smiling softly and said, "Just something simple. It may be a little worn, but there's beauty in things that aren't perfect."

Wilma tilted her head, her expression softening for a moment as she looked between the teacup and Ruth. "Yeah… maybe so."

They stood there, a small moment of unspoken understanding passing between them before Wilma broke the quiet. "Alright, then. You take your pretty teacup, and I'll grab this ridiculous hat."

With a playful sigh, Wilma slipped her arm through Ruth's,

smoothly tugging her further into the flea market's bustling maze. Ruth felt a bit stiff at first—physical touch wasn't something she was accustomed to, especially with someone outside her community.

But as they wandered past mismatched furniture and boxes of old books, she found herself silently asking *Gott* for understanding. She knew He must have a purpose even in this unexpected stop, and she prayed for peace with Wilma's boldness, her way of making light of the things that clearly weighed on her heart. There was a lesson here, she sensed, perhaps one in patience and grace, and Ruth reminded herself that sometimes the Lord placed opposites together for a reason.

As they made their way to the next stall, Ruth felt a warmth inside, content with the unexpected joy of the moment.

They moved along until Wilma spotted a rack of vintage hats, each one brighter and more extravagant than the last. With a mischievous look, she plucked a wide-brimmed leopard-print hat and plopped it onto Ruth's head, arranging the feather to sit just above her brow.

"Oh, Wilma, no..." Ruth began, blushing furiously, but Wilma was already adjusting it for her.

"Come on, Ruth! You look like a million bucks!" Wilma

laughed, spinning her around to see herself in a nearby mirror. Ruth caught sight of her reflection and, after a pause, burst out laughing too. She looked utterly ridiculous but didn't mind one bit.

They both stopped when Wilma's phone rang. Retrieving it from her pocket, she held up a finger to excuse herself when she saw Seth's name flashing across the screen. Ducking away from the bustling flea market crowd, she answered Seth's call, bracing herself for the warmth in his voice that she couldn't help but feel each time they spoke. "Hey, Seth," she said, her tone flat, but her heart lifting ever so slightly.

"Hey," he replied. "I just wanted to check in and see how you're doing out there."

"Still breathing, still trucking along," she joked, though her voice had a bit of an edge. "I'm digging through a mountain of junk just to find something worth keeping."

Seth laughed, and the sound was like a warm breeze, carrying the easy joy of memories. "Like last summer at the junk auction? You had that look in your eyes, convinced there was some hidden treasure under all those rusted tools and broken knick-knacks."

She chuckled, the memory pulling a reluctant smile to her

lips. "Hey, that old typewriter wasn't junk—it was vintage. And I almost had to wrestle that guy in overalls to win it."

"Yeah, and you were glowing like a kid on Christmas morning. It didn't matter that we spent hours sorting through other people's cast-offs; you found what you wanted."

There was a pause, the warmth of his words reaching her in a way she wasn't sure she could accept. "Maybe that's how I feel about you, Wilma," he said. "Even if you feel buried in the mess, I'm still here, hoping you'll find what you're looking for."

Her chest tightened, the weight of his words settling somewhere deep. A brief silence filled the space, her heart torn between appreciation and the protective wall she'd built. "We'll see, Seth. Maybe one of these days, I'll find my way out of this pile."

"And remember," he added, "you don't have to sort through it alone."

With a soft laugh, she added her usual sarcasm to lighten the mood. "Well, if I end up with another typewriter, I'll call you first."

Seth laughed; a sound filled with the steady patience that only made her ache more. "I'll be waiting. Typewriter or not."

They lingered a moment longer before she said goodbye, slipping her phone back into her bag. His words stayed with her, echoing like the memory of an almost-found treasure, buried but still within reach.

CHAPTER 10

As they left the misty hills of West Virginia behind and crossed into Virginia, the landscape stretched wide, rolling pastures dotted with trees and the occasional farmhouse slipping by. The sun climbed higher as Ruth sat back, enjoying the peaceful scene.

Wilma was unusually quiet, her gaze fixed ahead as she drove. Eventually, she broke the silence with a soft chuckle. "Did I ever tell you my dad was obsessed with history?" she said, her lips curving into a small smile. "Every year, he'd drag us down to Colonial Williamsburg. Said it would 'build character.'"

Ruth smiled, imagining a young Wilma trying to escape her dad's enthusiasm. "Sounds like he wanted you to see a little bit of the past."

"More like he wanted me to wear a colonial bonnet and appreciate churning butter," Wilma laughed, rolling her eyes.

"But the truth is, those were some of the best times… back when my mom was still with us. She was the glue. Everything fell apart after she died."

Ruth listened, sensing that even Wilma's light tone couldn't mask the sorrow under her words. She waited, letting Wilma lead the way.

Wilma's voice turned softer, almost hesitant. "And, you know, it's hard to believe in this grand 'plan' everyone talks about when the people you love get ripped away. Like, really, what kind of plan is that?"

Ruth glanced out the window, thinking of her own questions, her own uncertainties over the years. "I don't have an answer for that," she said. "Sometimes, when things have been hard, I just ask *Gott* to stay close. Even when I don't understand Him."

Wilma looked over, raising a brow. "So, basically, you're telling me to get chummy with the Big Guy, even though I'm mad at Him?"

Ruth chuckled, appreciating Wilma's knack for diffusing tension with humor. "Well, I don't think He's scared of our anger. And I don't think He minds if we don't understand everything. He's got big shoulders. Maybe it's enough to just tell Him how you feel."

Wilma let out a long sigh. "I don't know. It just feels weird. Like, 'Hi, God. I know I haven't been great at the whole religion thing, but could you maybe explain Yourself?'" She smirked, half-joking, half-serious. "I guess I've never been good at asking for help."

Ruth nodded, understanding. "Maybe that's why He put us on this road together—to help each other. Even if we're just figuring it out as we go."

Wilma smiled. "Alright," she said with a wry grin. "Guess I'll keep an open line, just in case He wants to explain Himself on this little road trip of ours."

As they drove closer to Williamsburg, Ruth's curiosity got the best of her. She glanced at a passing road sign and finally put two and two together. "Colonial Williamsburg… is that where we're headed?" she asked, a hint of excitement in her voice.

Wilma grinned, glancing over at Ruth. "You guessed it! I thought you'd enjoy it too. Plus, it's been forever since I've come back."

As they entered the visitor's center and made their way into the historical district, they immediately took in the sights of the charming Colonial buildings and actors strolling in period attire. The atmosphere buzzed with people, and Ruth couldn't help but admire the meticulously preserved environment.

Just then, a man approached, clearly mistaking Ruth for one of the 'staff.' "Pardon me, ma'am," he said politely, "could you point me toward the blacksmith shop? My kids can't wait to see it."

Ruth's cheeks turned a bit pink, and she glanced over at Wilma, who was already smirking. "Oh, um… I'm not…" Ruth stammered, caught off guard.

"Yes, *ma'am,* please do point us toward the blacksmith," Wilma chimed in, containing her laughter.

The man's face reddened as he realized his mistake. "Oh, I'm so sorry! I just thought… well, with your dress…"

Ruth smiled. "It's no trouble at all. I'm just as much a tourist as you are."

Once the man wandered off, Wilma gave Ruth a playful nudge. "You fit right in."

Ruth raised an eyebrow but couldn't help smiling. They both laughed, and as they walked through the streets, Wilma leaned closer, looking around kindheartedly. "You know, I didn't think anyone else could make this place feel so… well, like family. Thanks, Ruth. I wouldn't want to be here with anyone else."

Ruth's smile softened. "It's a blessing to be here with you too, Wilma."

As they wandered through the heart of the cobble-lined streets, Wilma's nose caught the unmistakable scent of fresh, warm apple pie mingling with the smoky aroma of roasted turkey and hearty stews. "Oh, Ruth, we have to eat here!" she said, guiding her toward a small tavern with a rustic sign swinging above the door.

Inside, they were greeted by a cozy room lit by flickering lanterns, with wooden tables and benches full of people enjoying hearty Colonial-style meals. They ordered coffee and a slice of the apple pie that had drawn Wilma in.

As the plate arrived, Wilma took a bite of the pie and closed her eyes, savoring the taste. "This... this tastes just like the apple pie my mom used to make." Her voice softened, and she looked over at Ruth with a wistful smile. "Every fall, she'd fill the house with the smell of baking pies, making each one from scratch. We'd all gather in the kitchen, and my dad would be sneaking bites of the crust as soon as they came out of the oven."

She laughed, the memory shining in her eyes. "Those weekends felt perfect, you know? Just the three of us, crowded around our little kitchen table with pie crumbs everywhere and my dad going on about how one day he'd make the perfect pie too. I'm not sure he ever did, but…" she trailed off, taking another bite, letting the warmth of the memory fill her.

Ruth smiled, watching Wilma as she remembered. "It sounds like such a beautiful memory. I think maybe those moments stick with us because they were so full of love."

Wilma nodded, swallowing past a lump in her throat. "I suppose so. I miss them both, and I guess I didn't expect to find a piece of them here today."

***

Back in their hotel room after a long day exploring, Ruth slipped into the bathroom to freshen up. The sounds of water running and gentle humming floated out as Wilma lay sprawled on her bed, flipping through the brochure they'd picked up on colonial crafts. When Ruth emerged, she had a small, almost shy smile on her face.

"What's up?" Wilma asked, looking at her curiously.

Ruth chuckled, a bit hesitantly. "I was just remembering something funny… something I probably shouldn't share, actually."

Wilma grinned, propping herself up on her elbows. "Now you have to tell me! Don't leave me hanging!"

Ruth shook her head, laughing gracefully as she took a seat across from Wilma. "Alright, fine. Well, after I healed from my surgery, I at last worked up the courage to step on the scale. I had this grand idea I'd lost some significant weight after everything." She chuckled. "Five pounds." Ruth stretched out her hand. "Five. I remember thinking, 'All that for just five pounds?'"

Wilma burst out laughing, the sound filling the room, and Ruth joined in, shaking her head at herself. "You wouldn't believe the fuss I made to Levi about it. Not that I'd ever admit it to anyone else—I mean, who cares about weight, right?" Ruth paused, giving Wilma a wry look. "But here I was, fussing over five pounds."

"Five pounds!" Wilma snickered, trying to keep a straight face. "That's almost worse than no pounds at all. Guess your body really likes you just the way you are."

Ruth's laughter softened, and she grew a bit reflective. "It got me thinking, though, about how our bodies are just temporary. You know, like a tent—just a place we stay in for a while. It's what the Bible says." She glanced at Wilma, unsure if her words would resonate.

But Wilma seemed genuinely interested. "A tent, huh? I actually like that idea," she said, her voice softer. "Like… all this stuff with our bodies isn't forever. That maybe there's something more."

Ruth nodded; her eyes gentle. "That's the way I see it. It helps me let go of a lot of fears. Because one day, this 'tent' of mine will be complete and whole again, in heaven. It's comforting, you know?"

Wilma leaned back, gazing at Ruth thoughtfully. "You really believe that?"

"I do," Ruth replied, her voice steady. "It's helped me feel okay with looking at myself these days. Who I am inside, what *Gott* sees, is so much more important than what I see."

Wilma took a deep breath. "That… makes sense. More sense than a lot of things I've been pondering lately."

As Wilma flipped off the light, darkness filled the room, a comforting stillness around them. She closed her eyes, and for the first time in some eighteen years, a few words of thanksgiving lingered on her lips.

Thank you… for this time with Ruth, she whispered in her heart, the words soft yet profound, almost foreign after so many silent years. It felt like reconnecting with a forgotten part of herself, like reaching out to someone she hadn't spoken to since her mother's passing.

In the bed next to hers, Ruth's gentle breathing created a steady rhythm, grounding Wilma in a way she hadn't felt in ages. She let herself relax, her mind lingering on the laughter, quiet moments, and small kindnesses they'd shared on this trip. As she drifted into sleep, she felt a spark of something new—a small, unexpected warmth in her heart that, just maybe, was the beginning of hope.

***

The following day, they crossed from Virginia into North Carolina, and the world around them transformed into an array of greens, with mountain ridges dotted by thick forests and rivers glimmering in the sun. Ruth took in the beauty of each turn, marveling at the sights and the warmth of the summer air filtering through the car windows.

A gentle beat played on the radio, and Ruth found herself listening a bit more intently than she had to anything on the trip thus far. She even caught herself tapping her fingers to the rhythm, an instinctive reaction she hadn't anticipated.

Wilma noticed, her lips quirking into a knowing grin. "You know, I think you might just like country music."

Ruth laughed, her cheeks coloring. "*Ach*, it's only the rhythm. I suppose it's catchy, is all." She folded her hands in her lap, hesitating before she added, "Levi would probably be raising an eyebrow right about now, thinking I've been exposed to a bit too much of the world."

Wilma chuckled, glancing over with a playful sparkle in her eye. "Maybe I'm a bad influence, dragging you into things like this. But it's kind of fun watching your reaction."

Ruth smiled, relaxing back into her seat. "I'm realizing that just because something is different doesn't make it bad." She paused, her gaze fixed on the road ahead. "There's a joy in seeing the world in a new way, even if it's not what I'm used to."

Ruth glanced over at Wilma with a curious smile as she maneuvered the winding road. "So, where are we off to today?"

Wilma grinned, her eyes sparkling with a hint of mystery. "I thought it'd be fun to go somewhere neither of us has been. I found this place online called the Fred W. Symmes Chapel, but some people just call it 'Pretty Place.' It's supposed to be up high on a mountain. I thought… well, it seemed like something you might enjoy."

Ruth's brows rose in surprise. "*Ach*, on top of a mountain? That does sound different. But what should we expect?"

Wilma shook her head, her excitement contagious. "I have no idea! I guess we'll both see when we get there."

As they drove, the narrow mountain road led them through forests of tall pines and maples, the sunlight filtering through the branches in shifting patches of golden light. The air grew cooler, carrying the clean, earthy scent of high mountain terrain, and the views opened up more and more with each twist in the road, revealing sweeping vistas of valleys and distant hills.

As they wound up the mountain road, Ruth chuckled agreeably, almost to herself.

"What's funny?" Wilma asked, glancing over with a grin.

"Oh, just thinking that if Levi knew where I was and what I've experienced along this trip so far, he might not have been so easy to convince," Ruth admitted, a playful glint in her eye.

Wilma laughed. "Well, I certainly didn't expect to have a good Amish woman as my travel buddy. But I have to ask… when you say 'convince,' is that because Levi has to, you know, *let* you do things? It sounds so old-fashioned."

Ruth considered her words, tucking a few stray hairs under her *kapp*. "*Jah*, I suppose it might sound that way. But it's not about 'letting' me, exactly. In our marriage, we rely on each other, and I respect his guidance just as he respects mine. We make decisions together, especially ones as big as this trip."

Wilma nodded, watching the road ahead thoughtfully. "I think Seth might appreciate that kind of give-and-take. He comes from a really strong Christian family. Sometimes I wonder if… if I'd ever measure up to what he hopes for in a marriage."

Ruth turned to her with a compassionate gaze. "You don't think you're enough for him?"

"More like, I don't know if I'll ever be able to give him what he wants," Wilma replied, her voice growing quiet.

"*Ach*," Ruth said, choosing her words carefully. "Maybe Seth sees something more in you than you see in yourself."

Wilma swallowed hard, her gaze dropping to her lap. "I don't know. Between my health and… my doubts about God, I can't help but think he deserves someone without all this baggage."

"But do you love him?"

The question settled in the car for a moment, heavy but tender. Wilma nodded slowly, almost as if it hurt to admit. "I do, but it doesn't feel fair to hold him back from the future he wants. Sometimes, it just feels easier to keep my distance. Safer."

Ruth gave her a reassuring nod. "Love isn't always safe. Sometimes it asks us to trust, even when we're scared."

They rode on in quiet reflection; the only sound was the hum of the engine and road under the tires. And then, as the mountain stretched higher before them, they saw it. A small, unassuming chapel perched on the edge of the ridge, its stone walls open to the sky and mountains beyond. Both women fell silent, their earlier conversation giving way to a shared awe as they approached the Fred W. Symmes Chapel, feeling something unspoken settle between them. For now, their journey was right here, side by side, as they faced both the beauty of the world and the questions it stirred within them.

When they pulled up to the small parking area, both women fell silent. The path led them to a cliffside, and there, just past the railing, was the simple stone chapel perched on the edge of the mountain, open to the endless expanse of sky and peaks beyond. The cross, set against a backdrop of rolling clouds and endless blue, made Ruth catch her breath.

"Look at that," Wilma whispered, taking a step closer to the edge, her voice filled with awe.

Ruth, equally moved, stepped up beside her. The place was almost too beautiful, like it was crafted straight from a dream. As they walked toward the chapel, the quiet seemed to magnify every sound—the rustle of leaves, the soft calls of birds echoing in the distance, and the gentle mountain breeze.

They took seats on one of the simple benches inside the chapel. For a few moments, they both just gazed out at the view, letting the peace of the place sink into their bones. The majesty of the mountains made the world seem both impossibly large and deeply intimate, like they'd found a space where God was undeniably present.

Wilma turned to Ruth; her expression vulnerable. "I don't know what it is about this place, but I feel like… like I've never felt before. Something bigger than anything I could've imagined. I can't quite explain it, but…" Her voice faltered, the words seeming to catch on some unnamed emotion.

Ruth nodded, leaned in and whispered, "That's *Gott's* presence."

Wilma let out a slow, trembling breath, her gaze fixed on the cross silhouetted against the mountains. She closed her eyes and whispered, almost to herself, *"God, if you're there… I think I might need you."*

As they pulled out of the parking lot, Wilma's gaze drifted to the rearview mirror reflecting to the chapel, its open stone walls silhouetted against the fading light. Her eyes misted over, a quiet ache settling in her chest. She didn't want to leave, didn't want to let go of the profound peace she'd felt within those walls. It was unlike anything she'd experienced, an overwhelming sense of something bigger than herself—of a presence that both knew her fears and held her close, even if she couldn't understand it.

"I don't want to leave." She murmured; her voice subdued.

Ruth smiled. "Sometimes the Lord touches our hearts in places we didn't even know were waiting for Him."

Wilma swallowed, the rawness of her emotions leaving her unsteady. "It's like… like I don't want to lose that feeling, but I don't know how to keep it. How do you… I mean, how do you carry that with you?"

Ruth was quiet for a moment, her hands resting on her lap. "His peace isn't something we can hold onto with our own strength. We just have to ask Him to fill us with it each day. Some days, it feels close, and some days, we have to remind ourselves that He's still there, even when we can't feel it."

CHAPTER 11

As they left the chapel in North Carolina and headed south toward Greenville, South Carolina, Wilma blinked a few times, trying to focus on the road ahead. A deep weariness settled over her, and she couldn't shake it, even though the drive wasn't particularly long.

Checking the map on her dashboard, she let out a small sigh of relief when she saw they had less than an hour left before reaching her friend Janel's home. She looked over at Ruth, offering a smile that she hoped masked her fatigue.

"You're going to love Janel," Wilma said, trying to keep her voice light. "She's gone all out for our stay. She said she'd show us around Greenville, or we can just lay low and rest... whatever we feel up to."

Ruth smiled, giving her seatbelt a slight adjustment as she settled in. "That sounds like a blessing. I'll admit, I could use a bit of a rest myself, and I can tell you need one too."

Wilma let out a small laugh, though her energy was fading. "Trust me, I feel like I could sleep for a week. Janel's hospitality couldn't have come at a better time."

After a quiet moment, Ruth asked, "How did you and Janel meet?"

A grin spread across Wilma's face as she recalled the memory. "College. She was my roommate, and from day one, we clicked. We've been inseparable since." She paused for a moment, her gaze drifting to the passing cars. "She's one of the few people in my life I can be real with. No holding back, no pretending. Janel is the real deal, the kind of friend who doesn't sugarcoat things. She tells me the truth, even when I don't want to hear it."

"That's a true friend for sure," Ruth replied, nodding thoughtfully.

"How about you?" Wilma asked, glancing Ruth's way. "Do you have a friend like that? Someone you can share anything with?"

Ruth was quiet for a moment, a look of reflection on her face before she spoke. "I did. Her name was Stella. She passed on years ago, and it left a big void in my life. She was the one person I could share anything with, someone who always pointed me back to our faith. Losing her was hard on all of us, especially Emma… Stella was her mother."

Wilma noticed the shift in Ruth's tone and felt a pang of sadness for her. "That must've been tough," she murmured, genuinely moved by Ruth's quiet strength.

Ruth's voice softened, and she glanced out the window, memories clearly surfacing as she continued. "When Stella passed, it felt like a piece of my heart went with her. Losing someone close… it changes you. In our community, we see death as part of *Gott's* plan, a doorway to eternity. But even with that comfort, I wasn't sure how I'd go on without her. If it weren't for the other women always checking on me… I don't know how I would have managed."

Wilma nodded, sensing the depth of Ruth's pain and resilience. Ruth continued, "What kept me going was knowing I could care for her daughter. When Emma married Samuel, I saw it as a way to honor Stella's memory—to step into her shoes a bit, to guide Emma like Stella would have, to offer a mother's love in her absence."

The quiet filled the car as Ruth gathered her thoughts before continuing. "Our life on this earth is fleeting, but it's not easy to see beyond the grief in those moments. Each day, I thank

Gott for giving me a way to honor Stella's memory by loving her daughter as if she were my own."

The openness in Ruth's words surprised Wilma. "Sounds like you're not just honoring her memory, you're keeping it alive in a way she'd be proud of."

Ruth's face softened with a small smile. "Maybe so. And maybe one day, I'll see her again. For now, I'll do my best to love those she left behind."

Wilma couldn't help but admire Ruth's faith, though she found it hard to relate to that level of trust. "You make it sound easy," she said, almost to herself.

"Oh, it's far from easy," Ruth replied, her voice steady but warm. "But it's a choice I make every day."

They rode in silence for a while, each lost in their own thoughts as the miles stretched on. The soft hum of the road beneath them was a comfort, lulling Ruth into a gentle sleep beside Wilma.

As they turned into Janel's familiar neighborhood, Wilma slowed, pulling carefully into the driveway. She took a moment to breathe deeply, steadying herself before waking Ruth. An overwhelming wave of fatigue washed over her, so intense it felt as if a heavy weight had settled over her entire body. Every inch of her ached, and even the simple act of lifting her arm felt daunting.

She glanced at Ruth, then reached over and lightly placed a hand on her shoulder. "Ruth. We made it," she whispered. "We're here."

Ruth stirred, blinking herself awake. Noticing the weariness in Wilma's eyes, she offered a sympathetic smile. "Let's get inside and rest," she said tenderly, her tone full of understanding.

Together, they gathered their belongings, each silently grateful for the chance to rest in the comfort of a friend's home.

As soon as they stepped inside, Ruth immediately noticed how Wilma's eyes were dull and exhausted, and her steps seemed heavier than usual. It didn't take more than a few minutes before Ruth suggested she lay down for a rest.

After a few words of gratitude, Wilma retreated to the guest room, leaving Ruth and Janel in the cozy living room. Janel offered Ruth a seat, her welcoming smile setting Ruth at ease.

"Can I get you some iced tea or anything?" Janel asked, settling into the armchair across from her.

"That would be lovely, thank you," Ruth replied, feeling

comforted by the beautiful space around her.

As Janel handed her a cool glass, she leaned forward with genuine curiosity. "So, Ruth, tell me a little about yourself. Wilma's spoken so highly of you, but I feel like I hardly know you."

Ruth chuckled, a bit taken aback. "Well, there's not much to tell. I've lived a quiet life in Pennsylvania. My husband, Levi, and I have raised our family there, surrounded by friends and family." She paused, looking thoughtful. "Life is simple, you could say, but it's fulfilling."

Janel smiled, taking a sip of her tea. "That sounds peaceful. I imagine it's quite different from Wilma's world."

"It is," Ruth admitted, glancing towards the hallway where Wilma had disappeared. "But she's shown me much about the world outside our community. Wilma's… a force, you might say. Bold and full of life."

Janel nodded, her expression softening. "She's certainly one of a kind. But I worry a little. She's not looking well, is she? I know she's been through a lot already, and sometimes I wonder if this trip was maybe a bit much for her."

Ruth paused, carefully choosing her words. "It's true. The journey seems to be taking its toll on her. But I think she needed this more than anything—a chance to step away from all the doctor visits and treatments, even if only for a short time."

Janel tilted her head, listening intently. "You seem to know her well. I think you're right. She's stubborn, though. Always has been, even back in college. She'd push herself to the edge rather than let anyone think she couldn't handle something."

Ruth nodded, her eyes softening. "It's part of why I agreed to come with her. She keeps her struggles close, but I see the weight of everything she's facing. I pray that, perhaps, through this journey, she'll find the peace she needs, or at least a bit of comfort along the way."

Janel looked down, swallowing hard before she met Ruth's gaze again. "I appreciate you looking after her. She needs someone like you in her life right now… someone who knows how to show her motherly love in a way every young woman needs."

Ruth nodded. "*Gott* has a purpose for all things. I'm here because it was meant to be, and I only hope to do whatever small thing I can."

Janel smiled, her eyes misting a bit. "Well, if anyone can do that, it's you."

***

Two days later, Janel guided Ruth and Wilma to Falls Park on the Reedy, an early morning trip meant to beat the South Carolina heat. As they stepped onto the stone paths leading toward the park, Ruth marveled at the sight before her. The Reedy River cascaded over smooth rocks, flowing beneath the graceful curves of a suspension bridge, while birds flitted from tree to tree along the shaded banks. The air was tinged with a hint of the summer warmth that would soon settle in.

They strolled leisurely, the city's quiet hum filling the background. Occasionally, a jogger passed by, their footsteps soft on the path, while early-morning families and tourists enjoyed the scenic walk. Downtown Greenville was beginning to stir: shops opening, the faint clink of silverware as cafés set out tables, and the smell of fresh coffee drifting from a nearby stand.

But before they had walked very far, Ruth noticed Wilma's steps slowing. Her breathing grew a bit heavier, and she rubbed the back of her neck, a small sign of fatigue that Ruth didn't miss.

"Let's sit for a moment," Ruth suggested, nodding to a

nearby park bench shaded by a sprawling oak tree.

Wilma sighed gratefully, lowering herself onto the bench. "I'd forgotten how humid it can get here," she admitted, wiping her forehead with the back of her hand.

Janel glanced at her friend with concern but kept her tone light. "That's why we're out here before the sun decides to put on its full show."

As they sat on the bench, Janel gave Wilma a gentle squeeze on the shoulder. "I'll go grab us some iced coffee from that café we passed. You two stay here and enjoy the view. I'll be right back."

Wilma smiled faintly, giving Janel a grateful nod. As Janel walked away, Ruth watched her friend's face, noticing the tiredness etched into her eyes and the way she held herself more delicately than usual.

They both sat quietly, letting the sounds of the falls fill the silence. Finally, Ruth turned to Wilma. "I wonder… maybe we ought to head back home after a few days here? You've done so much already, and it's clear you need rest."

Wilma's face tightened with determination, and she shook her head. "No, I promised you Florida, and that's where we're going. Pinecraft was all we talked about, and I can't turn back now."

Ruth tilted her head, a gentle but insistent look in her eyes. "I'm all right with whatever we decide. I know this trip means so much to you, but there will be other trips if you need this one to end early."

"Ruth," Wilma said, her voice firm but softened by the gentleness in Ruth's face, "we're not giving up. But I'll make a deal. No more detours. We'll go straight to Pinecraft, no extra stops. Deal?"

Ruth's lips curved into a soft smile. "Deal."

Wilma exhaled, a hint of relief crossing her face as she looked out at the water. "I need this, Ruth. I need to prove to myself that I can do this—that life hasn't completely decided my future."

Ruth reached over and patted Wilma's hand, letting her silence speak the words she held in her heart. As they sat there, waiting for Janel to return, Ruth leaned back, her gaze following the river as it wound its way around the park. "This place reminds me a bit of home, with all the greenery," she said, smiling. "But the sounds are different, and it's definitely hotter here than in Pennsylvania."

Wilma grinned. "It's something, isn't it? They've put so

much effort into keeping the park close to nature, even right in the middle of downtown."

Ruth gave a small nod, her gaze fixed on the flowing water. Ruth watched her, feeling the moment's stillness deepen, as she missed Levi and her home.

****

After packing up, Janel handed over the keys to her parents' Jekyll Island condo with a grin. "You two take your time getting to Pinecraft and enjoy a night at the beach," she said. "Drop the keys in the mail when you get back home, and please, rest up."

Wilma beamed, holding the keys up like a prize. "Janel, you're the best. And I didn't think you'd ever make a good roommate."

Janel laughed. "Just promise me you'll take it easy. Don't make me come looking for you two at the hospital in Pinecraft because you went overboard with adventure."

Ruth chuckled, nodding. "I'll make sure of it. Rest is exactly what we're looking for."

As they drove south on I-26 through the scenic stretch of South Carolina, the peaceful countryside seemed to pass in a blur. Wilma, lost in thought, tentatively broke the silence. "Do you ever think about what comes next? I mean, if… if everything goes okay?"

Ruth glanced over at her. "*Jah*, I do. I think about seeing my family grow, spending time with my grandchildren… even doing more trips like this. Why do you ask?"

Wilma shrugged, attempting a laugh. "Well, I try to think about it, but the future feels kind of murky these days. It's like everyone says I should be hopeful, and part of me is, but then there's this other part that's, well, let's just say it's not the pep-talk version of me."

Ruth smiled. "Sometimes the future can feel like a big, empty space, and we don't always know what will fill it. But that doesn't mean it can't be full of good things."

"Good things, huh?" Wilma rolled her eyes, smirking. "Well, as long as that includes staying out of hospitals and eating pizza without feeling like I ran a marathon just to pick it up, I'm game. Seriously, Ruth, what do you imagine for me?"

Ruth thought for a moment. "I imagine peace. And a sense of strength you might not see in yourself yet. And who knows? *Gott* might even surprise you."

"Yeah… I guess I can hope for that, can't I? Maybe even

picture myself doing something totally out of character, like—oh, I don't know—being a mother or something."

Ruth laughed. "I could see you doing something just like that. It's those little pictures of the future that help us hold on, even if they're not guaranteed."

They lapsed into silence as the highway stretched on, the trees and open fields rolling by. Wilma stared out the window, feeling a strange sense of peace, as if maybe, just maybe, there was room for more than just getting through each day. It was a thought she would hold on to, at least for now.

***

The sticky summer air clung to them as they sat, each with an iced coffee in hand. The humidity, thick and heavy even this early in the morning, wrapped around them like a warm blanket as they watched the sun inch up over the horizon. The Atlantic sparkled, reflecting the pinks and golds of dawn, and Ruth's wide-eyed stare never left the waves.

"Goodness, how do people stand this heat?" Ruth fanned herself with her hand, a smile playing on her lips. "I think I'm melting faster than butter on a hot griddle."

Wilma chuckled, brushing a strand of damp hair off her forehead. "Oh, believe me, you get used to it. Sort of. But hey, I have an idea…" She set her coffee on the small table and pointed toward the shoreline, grinning mischievously.

Ruth followed her gaze, eyes narrowing. "Now, don't you get any wild ideas. The ocean and I are only just making our introductions."

"Oh, come on!" Wilma said, laughing as she tugged on Ruth's arm. "You said you'd dip your toes in at least. And with this heat, I think a bit more than your toes might thank you!"

Ruth hesitated, glancing back toward the waves. "Well, I suppose a little cooling off wouldn't hurt."

Before Ruth knew it, Wilma had taken her hand, and they were padding down the wooden steps off the porch of their condo and onto the sandy path leading to the beach. Ruth's feet sank into the warm sand, and she couldn't help but giggle, partly from the heat and partly from the sheer thrill of it all.

"Alright, here goes nothing," Ruth muttered, stepping into the shallow surf. The water lapped up around her ankles, warm from the sun yet cool enough to offer relief from the muggy air.

"See?" Wilma grinned, wading in up to her knees. "Not so bad, right?"

Ruth laughed, lifting her skirt a little higher as a larger wave swept in, splashing her calves. "It's delightful!"

By the time they returned to the porch, Ruth's skirt was damp at the edges and both their faces flushed from both laughter and the humidity, they collapsed into their chairs with a contented sigh.

"Unexpected, but entirely worth it," Ruth said, a smile lingering on her face as she glanced at Wilma.

"That's what I'm here for," Wilma replied, lifting her glass in a playful toast. "Here's to more unexpected fun."

Ruth clinked her mug against Wilma's, feeling lighter than she had in a long time. Despite the heat, the humidity, and the early hour, it was a morning she'd never forget—one where friendship, laughter, and the gentle lap of the waves had turned the Georgia heat into a memory she'd cherish forever.

As they settled back onto the porch, still chuckling from their ocean antics, Wilma looked over at Ruth, taking in her long skirt and head covering with a grin.

"Girl, I don't know how you're not dying in that outfit," Wilma teased, fanning herself. "I'm in shorts, and I feel like I'm roasting alive!"

Ruth tugged at the hem of her skirt, smoothing it over her

knees. "*Ach*, I suppose I'm used to it. But I'll admit, this humidity is more than I bargained for." She glanced down at Wilma's breezy attire, raising an eyebrow. "Must be nice to feel the breeze on your legs."

"It's glorious," Wilma said, stretching out and playfully extending a leg. "Maybe I should find you a pair of shorts."

Ruth laughed, shaking her head. "I'm not sure the *Bishop* would take too kindly to that!"

"Oh, but can you imagine?" Wilma teased. "Ruth Yoder, the Amish trendsetter in bright pink shorts."

They both laughed, and Ruth shook her head, still smiling. "I think that might be too bold, even for me."

With the sun now fully rising, they both sighed and took in the view, the laughter between them adding a warmth that somehow made the heat feel more bearable. Ruth looked at Wilma, her eyes soft with gratitude. "You certainly know how to bring out a side of me I didn't know was there."

"Maybe that's the whole point of this trip," Wilma said, giving her a gentle nudge. "For both of us."

CHAPTER 12

As the car meandered through the narrow streets of Pinecraft, Ruth marveled at the neighborhood's quaint charm. This little Amish and Mennonite community, nestled within the hustle of Sarasota, felt like a world apart. The houses, each painted in soft pastel tones, seemed to exude a quiet warmth. Palm trees swayed in the humid evening breeze, while vibrant hibiscus flowers lined the sidewalks. light.

When they passed Pinecraft Park, Ruth's eyes were drawn to the beauty of Phillippi Creek, framed by ancient oak trees draped in Spanish moss.

Wilma stopped the car in front of Ruth's aunt Catherine's house. The cheerful coastal-blue home was surrounded by a neat white picket fence while hanging baskets of bright pink petunias swayed from the porch.

Ruth briefly noticed Wilma's pale complexion as she leaned heavily against the steering wheel. Her usual energy was missing, replaced again by a quiet weariness. "I'll get our things out of the trunk," Ruth said, already stepping out of the car. Wilma didn't protest; she simply nodded as she opened the door.

Catherine emerged from the house, her flip-flops making soft claps against the cement porch. "Ruth! You're a sight for sore eyes," she greeted warmly, enveloping Ruth in a brief hug before turning to Wilma. "And you must be Wilma. Ruth's told me all about you. Come in, you both look like you've had quite the journey."

Wilma managed a faint smile, but when she stepped out of the car, her movements were sluggish. Ruth noted how Wilma leaned on the car for support, her breath shallow. By the time they reached the porch, Wilma was visibly struggling.

Inside, the house was cool, the tile floor a soothing contrast to the heat that clung to their skin. Wilma slipped off her shoes and sighed as the cool surface met her bare feet. "This feels amazing," she murmured, her voice was faint, like a distant echo.

Ruth watched as Wilma's hand drifted to her forehead, her expression distant. Fever, Ruth thought silently, her heart tightening with concern. Before Catherine could offer a tour,

Wilma excused herself. "If you don't mind, I think I'll lie down for a bit," she said, her words tinged with fatigue.

"Of course, child," Catherine said kindly, pointing toward the guest room. "You get some rest. We'll get better acquainted later."

Wilma gave a slight nod and made her way down the hall, her steps unsteady. Ruth's eyes followed her until she disappeared into the room, then she turned to Catherine with a worried look.

"She's not well," Ruth admitted quickly. "I hoped this trip would be good for her, but now… I wonder if I made the right decision bringing her here."

Catherine placed a reassuring hand on Ruth's arm. "You did what you thought was best, Ruth. Let's give her a few days to rest and recover. Pinecraft has a way of soothing the soul."

Ruth nodded, but as she helped Catherine bring in their bags, her heart remained heavy with concern.

***

Ruth and Catherine settled on the front porch, the shuffleboard paddles clapping rhythmically in the park across the street. It was the kind of evening that invited quiet reflection, and Ruth welcomed the stillness after their long journey.

Catherine handed Ruth a glass of meadow tea. "It's good to have you here. I can tell this trip is more than just a visit."

Ruth nodded, her gaze drifting toward the park. "*Jah*, it is. Wilma… she's been through so much. Losing her mother so young and facing this illness on her own. It's left a hole in her heart. I feel *Gott's* hand in bringing us together, like He's asking me to step into that gap, to be there for her in a way her mother would."

Catherine leaned back in her chair. "It's a special bond you've formed. I can see how she looks to you, even when she tries to hide her vulnerability."

Ruth smiled. "She reminds me of myself when I was younger—headstrong, determined not to show weakness. But underneath, I can see how much she craves stability and guidance. She hides behind jokes a good bit, but I know she's searching for acceptance."

Catherine sipped her tea before adding, "It takes a strong person to walk through what Wilma's facing. But it also takes someone like you to remind her she doesn't have to walk alone."

Ruth exhaled deeply, her hands resting in her lap. "I pray every day that I'm doing right by her. I want her to see that *Gott* hasn't abandoned her, even in this storm."

Catherine set her chair in motion with the ball of her foot and added. "You're planting seeds. Whether she realizes it now or later, your love and faith are helping her grow."

Ruth nodded, feeling a quiet reassurance settle over her. "It's funny," she said, her tone lighter. "I never imagined myself on a road trip like this, especially with someone so different from me. But Wilma's shown me a side of life I might have never seen, and for that, I'm grateful."

Catherine chuckled. "Life has a way of surprising us. Sometimes, it's those unexpected connections that bring the greatest joy."

They sat in comfortable silence for a moment, the shuffleboard game winding down as twilight crept in. The air was rich with the scents of blooming jasmine and the faint smell of the brackish water of Phillippi Creek.

"Wilma's lucky to have you."

Ruth smiled, her heart swelling with a quiet hope. "I'm the one who's blessed. Every step of this journey, I feel *Gott* teaching me as much as He's guiding her."

***

Wilma stirred beneath the soft cotton blanket, her body heavy with exhaustion. The fever that had soundlessly settled over her in the night now clung to her like the Florida humidity, making every movement feel sluggish. She blinked slowly, her gaze shifting toward the doorway where a faint, soothing melody drifted in.

Ruth's voice carried kindly through the air, a hymn soft and familiar. The tune tugged at a corner of Wilma's memory, and she closed her eyes, letting it transport her back to her childhood. Her mother used to hum the very same melody while preparing dinner or tucking her into bed. The ache of longing nestled deep in her chest, but for once, it wasn't painful... just a quiet reminder of love.

Her consciousness slipped into a dream-like state. In the haze, she saw Seth standing beneath the branches of a large oak tree, pushing a small girl on a wooden swing. The child's laughter rang out, light and pure, as her dark curls bounced with every push. Wilma watched from afar, a spectator to a scene of life and joy.

A soft voice spoke behind her, startling her in the dream. *You can continue to watch from afar or trust Me to embrace the life I've planned for you. It's your choice.*

She didn't turn around; she didn't need to. The words weren't accusatory or harsh, they were filled with tenderness and hope. The peace they brought washed over her, settling her anxious heart. Her focus returned to Seth, whose face radiated warmth and contentment as he steadied the swing.

The scene shifted somewhat. Seth scooped the little girl into his arms, spinning her around before setting her down. He knelt, brushing the hair from her face, his eyes filled with fatherly love. Wilma felt her breath hitch, the image stirring something deep within her… a longing not for what was lost, but for what could be.

Her fevered mind wavered between dream and reality. Ruth's hymn filtered back in, grounding her as she slipped in and out of sleep. The vision of Seth and the child lingered even as her eyes fluttered open briefly. She heard Ruth's voice still singing, steady and unwavering, a beacon of comfort in the storm.

In that moment, Wilma whispered silently, her heart finding

words she hadn't spoken in years: *Help me trust You, Lord. I'm tired of standing on the sidelines.*

As sleep reclaimed her, a fragile but growing calm wrapped around her, soothing the restless spirit that had battled for control for so long.

***

Ruth carefully pushed open Wilma's bedroom door, her heart sinking at the sight before her. Wilma lay motionless, her face pale except for the unnaturally rosy flush on her cheeks. Her breathing was shallow, her body limp.

"Wilma?" Ruth whispered, stepping closer. She placed her hand on Wilma's forehead, feeling the intense heat radiating from her skin and her inability to rouse her. Panic gripped her.

"Catherine!" she called out, her voice cracking. Catherine hurried in, her face growing pale as she took in Wilma's state.

"She's burning up," Ruth said, her voice trembling. "We need help."

Within minutes, the wail of sirens pierced the air, and the paramedics arrived. One paramedic began taking Wilma's vitals while his partner hurriedly assessed her condition as Ruth told them about Wilma's recent diagnosis and treatment plan.

"We'll need to transport her." the paramedic asked, glancing up at Ruth. "You can ride with her."

Ruth barely registered Catherine's reassuring squeeze on her arm as she climbed into the ambulance. She sat beside Wilma, her hands tightly clasped together, silently praying. *Lord, be with her. She's in Your hands now.*

The female paramedic worked swiftly, inserting an IV and administering fluids. "Her blood pressure is dangerously low, likely due to a chemo-related infection," she explained, glancing at Ruth. "We'll know more once they run tests at the hospital."

Ruth nodded; her eyes fixed on Wilma's pale face. She reached out and kindly took her friend's hand. "Hang in there, Wilma," she whispered.

As they sped through traffic, Ruth felt an overwhelming sense of responsibility. She leaned closer and silently prayed. *Gott, protect her. Give her the strength she needs. She's not done fighting.*

When they arrived at the hospital, the medical team whisked Wilma away, leaving Ruth to pace the waiting room. Hours passed before a nurse showed her to Wilma's room. She entered the quiet room, her steps slow and deliberate. Sitting beside Wilma's bed, Ruth bowed her head, offering one more prayer for Wilma's healing.

She sat by Wilma's bedside, her eyes fixed on the monitors that displayed an array of beeping numbers and blinking lights for what seemed like hours. The sterile hospital room felt both too quiet and oppressively loud. Every now and then, a nurse would enter to check Wilma's vitals or adjust her IV, but otherwise, it was just Ruth and the soft hum of medical machinery.

Finally, a doctor entered, clipboard in hand, his expression serious. Ruth straightened in her chair, her heart quickening.

"She's stable, but her condition is serious," he began. "It's good you brought her in when you did, but frankly, she should've come in as soon as she started feeling unwell. The chemotherapy has weakened her immune system, and her body is struggling to fight off what appears to be a severe infection. We're treating her aggressively, but only time will tell how she responds."

Ruth's stomach clenched. "How long will she need to stay?"

"I can't answer that," the doctor replied. "We'll monitor her closely. These next twenty-four to forty-eight hours are critical."

As the doctor left, Ruth's gaze returned to Wilma. Her friend looked so small and fragile, a stark contrast to her usual vibrant self. Ruth took Wilma's hand, her voice hovered just above silence. "I'm here, Wilma. You're not alone."

A nurse entered, her eyes softening as she noticed Ruth's worry. "Are you family?" she asked.

Ruth hesitated only for a moment before nodding firmly. "I'm the only family she has right now."

The nurse looked serious. "If she has any other you might want to call them in."

Once the room was quiet again, Ruth leaned in closer to Wilma, her voice filled with quiet determination. "You've got a lot of people who care about you, Wilma. Stay with us… you have so much to live for."

She thought back to their journey—the laughter, the conversations, the shared moments of vulnerability. This young woman had become like a daughter to her, and now, watching her fight through this battle, Ruth felt the weight of her own words settle in her heart. She whispered a prayer, asking *Gott* for strength, not just for Wilma but for herself as well.

Lord, guide her through this storm. She's stronger than she knows, but she needs Your hand to steady her.

Ruth tucked the blanket up under Wilma's chin. They might not share blood, but in this moment, Ruth was every bit the family Wilma needed.

Ruth stepped into the hallway and approached the nurse's station. "May I use the phone?" she asked kindly. The nurse nodded and guided her to a small room. The landline sat on the desk, an ordinary object that suddenly felt like a lifeline.

Ruth hesitated, her hand hovering over the receiver. She dialed the familiar number to the phone in the farm shed, the community phone back home, and listened to the long rings echo in her ear. On the tenth ring, Levi's steady voice at last answered.

"Ruth?" he asked, concern lacing his tone.

"It's me," she said, her voice trembling a little. "Wilma's taken a turn, Levi. She's very sick. The doctors are hopeful but suggested I call in her family. I think her Seth needs to be here."

There was a pause on the other end as Levi absorbed her words. "What do you need me to do?"

Ruth closed her eyes, relieved by his calm response. "I need you to find him. I don't know exactly where he is, but someone in the community might. He needs to know what's going on and get to Sarasota as soon as he can."

"Consider it done. I'll find him, and I'll make sure he gets there."

"*Denki*," Ruth whispered, her voice thick with emotion. "I don't know what I'd do without you."

After hanging up, Ruth took a moment to steady herself before returning to Wilma's room. She sat once more by her side, taking her hand in her own. "Help is on the way, Wilma," she whispered. "*Gott* has a plan for you, and you won't face this alone."

She leaned back, offering silent prayers for strength and guidance, trusting that everything would unfold as it should.

***

The next evening, Ruth sat vigil by Wilma's side, her fingers clasped around the young girl's frail hand. Wilma drifted in and out of consciousness, her soft murmurs often calling for Seth. Each time, Ruth leaned in, whispering reassurances and silently praying for her friend's strength to return.

As the door creaked open, Ruth looked up and immediately knew who had arrived. Seth's presence filled the room, his deep concern etched on his face. His dark hair was damp, pushed back from his forehead with the back of his hand. His olive-toned skin seemed to contrast sharply against Wilma's pale complexion, a stark reminder of how much life had been drained from her over the past few weeks.

He nodded toward Ruth, his voice low and steady. "Thank you for sending for me," he said, his eyes never leaving Wilma.

Ruth stood, offering a small, warm smile. "She's been asking for you," she said delicately, stepping aside to give him her chair. Seth took the seat without hesitation, his hands quickly replacing Ruth's on Wilma's.

As Ruth calmly gathered her things, she glanced back once more. The way Seth gazed at Wilma spoke volumes, his love and devotion unmistakable. Ruth felt a deep sense of peace as she left the room, her role in this moment fulfilled. She had been the steady presence Wilma needed, but now it was time for Seth to take his place.

Walking down the quiet hospital corridor, Ruth offered a silent prayer of gratitude. *Thank you, Gott, for bringing him here. Please guide them both through this storm.*

She found a quiet corner in the waiting room, letting herself rest for the first time in hours, her heart lighter knowing Wilma was in the care of someone who loved her deeply.

CHAPTER 13

The soft hum of the hospital's machines faded into the background as Wilma's mind drifted into an otherworldly quiet. She found herself standing barefoot on a sandy beach, the horizon stretched endlessly before her, and in the distance, she could see a lone figure standing near the waterline.

As she took her first step toward him, her feet felt heavy, as though the sand beneath her was clinging to her every move. The closer she tried to get, the more resistant the ground seemed, but the figure ahead remained still, waiting.

"Wilma…" The voice was familiar, tender yet strong, and it pulled her forward despite the weight holding her back.

"Seth?" she whispered, the sound scarcely audible over the gentle crashing of waves.

The figure turned, and there he was, standing with his hand outstretched toward her. His dark hair tousled by the wind, his skin glowing under the sunlight. A bittersweet smile crossed his face as he beckoned her forward.

She tried to call out to him again, but her voice caught in her throat. "I want to reach you, but I'm so tired," she admitted, her words heavy with exhaustion and fear.

Seth's voice carried across the distance, steady and encouraging. "You don't have to do this alone, my love. Just take one step at a time."

She tried to move her legs, summoning every ounce of strength within her, and took another step, then another. Her heart ached with the longing to be near him, but with each stride, the fatigue in her soul seemed to weigh heavier.

He took a step closer, his voice warm and patient. "I'll be here, no matter how long it takes."

As she continued walking, the distance between her and Seth slowly closed. Though her legs trembled with every step, she pressed on, her fear and doubt gradually giving way to a fragile but growing hope.

Finally, as she reached out her hand toward Seth's, the dream began to dissolve, the soft crashing of waves replaced by the rhythmic beeping of a heart monitor and the weight of a hand over hers.

Wilma's eyes fluttered open for a brief moment. Her lips

moved, barely audible, "Seth…"

Sitting beside her, Seth leaned closer, his eyes never leaving her pale face. "I'm here, my love."

***

The chilled hospital room gave little comfort to Seth, who sat quietly, his fingers wrapped around Wilma's frail hand. The dim light from the overhead fixtures shone delicately across her face, accentuating her paleness but also the peaceful stillness in her features. For a moment, Seth allowed himself to believe she was resting, her body regaining strength bit by bit.

Then, a faint movement. Her eyelashes fluttered faintly, followed by the softest murmur of his name.

"Seth?" Her eyes opened just enough to see his face. Her voice, weak and a mere breath of a sound carried a weight of vulnerability. "You're here."

"I'm not going anywhere," he replied, his tone filled with emotion. "I told you I'll always be here."

A shadow of regret flickered across her face. "I'm sorry," she murmured. "I didn't want you to see me like this… "

Seth squeezed her hand lightly, his gaze never leaving hers.

"I see you and love every part of you, even now. Especially now."

Her lips trembled into the faintest smile, though her eyes glistened with unshed tears. She nodded weakly, her breath shallow. "I love… "

"You're my world, Wilma, please stay with me."

Her eyes began to close again, her strength waning, but not before she whispered, "… you."

As her breathing steadied, and she slipped back into unconsciousness, Seth leaned back, a mixture of relief and heartache washing over him. He softly kissed her knuckles, whispering, "Please stay with me my love."

***

Seth entered the waiting room, his footsteps dragging under the weight of the worry that clenched tight in his chest. Ruth was seated by the window, her hands neatly clasped, her eyes trained on the darkened sky beyond.

He approached peacefully and sat beside her, the silence between them almost reverent. For a moment, neither spoke.

"She's still asleep," Seth said; his voice was quiet, barely breaking the stillness.

Ruth turned to him with a gentle nod. "She needs rest, and so do you."

Seth shook his head. "I can't rest. Not when I know she's fighting so hard."

Ruth sighed. "She's strong-willed, *jah*, but that strength comes from a place of fear. She's trying to carry the burden alone, but even the strongest need help."

Seth leaned forward; his hands clasped tightly. "I've prayed for her every day... begged God to show her she doesn't have to fight this battle alone. When your husband came to my door, I thought… maybe this was an answer to my prayers."

Ruth nodded and replied, "Sometimes, our prayers aren't answered in the way we expect. You may not see the change right away, but your presence, your prayers—they matter."

Seth swallowed hard, nodding slowly. "I just don't know what more I can do."

Ruth's expression softened. "You're already doing it. She needs to see that your love isn't conditional to her health."

Seth looked up, his eyes searching hers. "But how do I show her that without pushing her further away?"

Ruth gave him a small, thoughtful smile. "Patience and

prayer. Keep showing her you're here, even when she tries to pull back. And Seth…" She paused; her voice gentle but firm. "Don't underestimate the power of quiet strength. Sometimes, just sitting with someone in their pain speaks louder than any words."

For a while, they sat together in silence, the quiet hum of the hospital filling the space. Seth found comfort in Ruth's steady presence, feeling a renewed sense of purpose as he prepared to continue his vigil by Wilma's side.

****

On the fifth morning, sunlight streamed through the hospital window on Wilma's pale face as her eyes fluttered open. Ruth noticed immediately and leaned forward; her expression filled with quiet relief.

"You're awake," she said softly, her voice carrying the weight of three long days of waiting.

Wilma offered a weak smile. "I felt you here."

Seth, sitting nearby, squeezed her hand. "We weren't going anywhere," he said, his eyes reflecting both exhaustion and relief.

Wilma shifted a tad, her gaze drifting to Ruth. "I had dreams," she began, her voice scarcely above a whisper as she turned toward Seth. "You were there… "

Seth nodded; his eyes warm. "God often meets us in those quiet places."

There was a long pause before Wilma spoke again, her tone uncertain. "… I saw Jesus."

Ruth smiled. "Your heart's been reaching out to Him. I can only imagine he'd come to you."

Wilma's brows furrowed slightly.

Ruth chuckled daintily. "He's always listening. Always watching. Always waiting for you to call on Him."

The room grew quiet again, but it was a comforting silence this time. Wilma closed her eyes and drifted off to sleep once again.

Ruth gave Wilma's arm a gentle squeeze, her gaze shifted to Seth, whose hopeful expression had softened the deep worry lines etched into his forehead.

***

The August heat wrapped around them as Seth navigated

the crowded parking lot at Siesta Key Beach. The salty air teased Wilma's scarf, and Ruth clutched her skirt, bracing against a playful breeze as they stepped onto the warm, soft sand. Voices of beachgoers mingled with the sound of crashing waves, creating a symphony of summer life.

Seth led them to a shaded spot beneath a large striped umbrella. "Right here… best view in the house," he said, laying out the blankets and chairs.

Ruth sank onto the blanket, her eyes drawn to the endless blue expanse of the ocean. "It's even more breathtaking than I imagined," she said, her voice full of awe.

Wilma smiled, easing into her chair. "A month ago, I wouldn't have believed I'd be here, let alone feeling this good."

"It's amazing what a few changes can do," Ruth said, turning to her. "You've embraced a whole new way of living."

Wilma chuckled. "Who knew you'd be the one to teach me about kale smoothies and the healing power of sunlight? If you'd told me back in Pennsylvania that I'd be eating quinoa and loving it, I would've laughed you right out of my apartment."

Ruth smiled warmly. "*Gott* provides wisdom in ways we don't always expect. Whole foods and sunshine have helped me feel stronger since my surgery. It's not just about avoiding certain foods, it's about nourishing the body He gave us."

Wilma nodded. "I have to admit, I feel better physically. It's like giving my body a fighting chance. But it's also given me mental clarity… and peace." She glanced at the ocean, the waves mirroring the rhythm of her newfound calm.

They shared a quiet moment, watching the tide. The breeze tugged at Ruth's dress, and Wilma let out a content sigh. "I think I needed this trip more than I realized. Not just for my health, but for my soul."

Ruth smiled and replied, "Healing happens in layers. Body, mind, and spirit."

Before Wilma could respond, Seth returned, holding three bottles of cold water. "Alright, ladies, you both look way too serious for a beach day."

Wilma took her bottle, smiling up at him. "Serious? We were just having a profound moment about kale and sunshine. You missed out."

Seth grinned, raising his water. "Here's to kale, sunshine, and making it through these last few weeks."

Wilma clinked her bottle against his. "To the journey… and to Ruth, for keeping me on track."

As they sipped their water, the sun dipped lower, painting the sky with streaks of pink and gold. Wilma looked around, taking in the scene—the laughter of families, the soothing sound of the waves, and the steady presence of her two closest companions.

"I'm ready for the next chapter," she said serenely, more to herself than to anyone else. But Ruth heard her, offering a knowing smile as she replied, "And I'm ready to go home."

CHAPTER 14

Ruth stepped into the familiar warmth of her kitchen, her heart swelling at the sight of Emma and Katie bustling about, preparing a homecoming dinner. The scent of freshly baked bread mingled with the sound of baby coos and the happy clatter of little feet scampering underfoot. Ruth couldn't help but pause for a moment to take it all in.

Katie was the first to notice her, wiping her flour-dusted hands on her apron. "*Mamm*! Look at you! All sun kissed and glowing. That Florida sunshine must've done wonders."

Ruth chuckled, rubbing the bridge of her nose. "Too much sun, perhaps, but oh, the ocean! It stretches forever, and the sand… it's like walking in flour. Siesta Key was a sight to behold."

Emma laughed, stirring a pot of stew. "*Jah*, that sun is sneaky. I remember Pinecraft. I practically bathed in sunscreen. Still came back with a few extra freckles."

Just then, Levi entered, his broad frame filling the doorway. His eyes softened as they met Ruth's, and he crossed the room in a few strides to pull her into a warm embrace. "It's good to have you home again. This place just isn't the same without you."

Ruth leaned into his embrace. "It's good to be back. After a day's rest, I'll be ready to jump back into things."

As she sat down, Emma's twin boys scrambled onto her lap, full of questions. "Where were you, *Grossmommi*? And why aren't there any cookies in the jar?"

Ruth laughed, kissing their cheeks. "*Ach*, I'll fill that jar soon enough, but let's save room for tonight's supper, hmm?"

Emma redirected them. "Off you go, boys. Let *Grossmommi* rest. And you've had enough treats today."

Once the boys ran off, Ruth turned to baby Daniel Jr., nestled in the daybed. "And look at you, little one. How you've grown!"

Katie sighed, brushing a stray hair from her face. "He should be. It feels like he's eating every two hours. Between him and the bakery, I've hardly kept up."

Ruth picked up Daniel in her arms, her voice soothing. "Well, now I'm home. I'll help where I can. I've had enough rest to last me a while."

Levi pulled up a chair beside her, his face thoughtful. "How's Wilma?"

"She's had a rough go. Her health took a scary turn for a few days, and there were moments when I wondered if she'd pull through. But *Gott* is good, and He's given her strength. She's on the mend now, preparing for her surgery."

She paused for a moment before adding. "Her surgery and healing will be more trying than what I endured. But she's ready."

Katie rested her hand on her mother's. "The Lord is with her, just as He was with you."

Emma nodded. "He uses even the hardest seasons to show His glory, *jah*?"

Ruth smiled. "*Jah* and it's a privilege to see His hand in Wilma's journey, and I trust that He will continue to guide her."

*****

Wilma switched the phone to her other ear, tucking herself further into the corner of the couch. "Ya know, Janel, I keep telling myself this should be a no-brainer, but here I am, waffling like I'm at an all-you-can-eat breakfast bar."

Janel's laugh was light on the other end. "Well, if it were me, I'd probably be right there with you, debating every option like it's the most important menu choice of my life. But seriously, have you talked to Seth about how you're feeling?"

Wilma groaned. "We've kind of danced around it. He's Mr. Supportive, all 'whatever you decide, I'm here for you.' Which is sweet, but let's be real. That's not helping me narrow down my choices." She paused, her voice softening. "There are just so many things to think about, and I don't want to spend the next year in and out of reconstruction surgeries."

Janel let a moment pass before speaking. "It's a lot, and no one's expecting you to have all the answers right away. But have you prayed about it? Like, really asked God for direction?"

Wilma laughed, though there wasn't much humor in it. "Oh, I've prayed, alright. But guess what? No booming voice, no burning bush. Just crickets."

Janel's tone shifted. "It's not about getting a neon sign from the sky. Sometimes, God's answer is in the peace you feel about a decision, even if it's not immediate. Have you felt any moments of calm, even just a little?"

Wilma ran a hand through her hair—or rather, where her

short hair started growing back. "I don't know. Maybe. There's so much noise in my head, it's hard to tell. One minute, I think I'm okay with skipping reconstruction, and the next, I'm worrying about how I'll feel when I look in the mirror."

Wilma stretched her legs out and stared at the ceiling. "I mean, it's not just about how I look. What if I hate the result? I'm a total mess!"

"I get it," Janel said. "It's overwhelming, and it's okay to feel that way. And I'll keep praying for you too. You're not alone in this. Not by a long shot."

Wilma shifted on the couch, tucking her feet beneath her and cradling the phone closer. "You're not going to believe this. Seth wants to get married. Like, before the surgery."

There was a brief pause, followed by Janel's incredulous laugh. "What? In a week? Is he insane or just hopelessly romantic?"

"Probably both," Wilma muttered, a small smile tugging at her lips. "He's all, 'Let's have a quick wedding, take a weekend honeymoon, and then face this surgery together.' He thinks it'll give me something good to focus on."

Janel's laughter softened, replaced by genuine curiosity. "And what do you think? Is your heart racing with excitement, or are you planning to strangle him with a wedding veil?"

"I mean, who does that? A week to plan a wedding, Janel! I'm just barely managing to wrap my head around surgery, let alone cake flavors and centerpieces." Wilma exhaled heavily. "But here's the thing… part of me loves the idea. It's so Seth, wanting to dive into life headfirst. He's trying to anchor me to something hopeful. And honestly? The thought of not doing this alone… it's kind of tempting."

Janel hummed thoughtfully. "Sounds like he's trying to create a moment of joy before things get tough. But what about you? Do you feel ready for marriage and all the emotional weight it brings on top of what you're already carrying?"

Wilma bit her lip, considering. "That's the problem. I don't know. Seth's been solid through all this, but I keep thinking, 'Is it fair to drag him into my storm?' What if he ends up resenting me later?"

"Resent you?" Janel's voice sharpened with disbelief. "Wilma, Seth's a grown man making his own choices. If he wants to be there for you, let him. Stop deciding for him. Besides, life's storms don't last forever."

Wilma chuckled dryly. "Storm metaphors now? What's next, a sermon?"

"You'd love it," Janel teased. "But seriously, you've got to stop carrying this weight alone. If Seth is offering to be your partner, why not lean on him? And as for planning a wedding in a week—who needs elaborate details? Just grab some flowers, pick a dress, and let the people who love you do the rest."

Wilma sighed, the tension in her shoulders easing just a little. "You make it sound so simple."

"Because it can be," Janel said warmly. "Focus on what really matters. Love, commitment, and faith in whatever comes next."

Wilma twirled a loose thread on her throw blanket, her voice softer now. "I'll think about it. But don't expect me to let him off the hook with the whole honeymoon idea. I'm not exactly honeymoon material right now."

"Don't sell yourself short," Janel replied. "Besides, the real honeymoon is just being with someone who makes you feel whole. Wherever you go, that's the destination."

A small laugh escaped Wilma. "That's cheesy even for you."

"Call it cheesy, but it's true." Janel's voice held a smile. "Now, if you decide to pull this off, you know I'll be there in a heartbeat."

"Thanks, Janel. I might need you to remind me of all this when I'm panicking about vows and veils."

"Anytime," Janel replied. "And remember—you don't have to wait for peace to fall from the sky. Sometimes, you have to take a step toward it."

Wilma nodded, even though Janel couldn't see her. "Got it. Step toward peace. And maybe Seth too."

***

The scent of freshly baked strawberry pies mingled with the warm cinnamon from the pastries cooling on the racks. Ruth moved her hands steadily as she worked the counter. The hum of the bakery's activity usually brought her peace, but today, a nagging unease stirred within her.

The bell above the door jingled, and her friends Susan and Esther entered, their greetings warm but tinged with concern. They gathered near the counter, their voices lowering as the conversation approached her health.

"Ruth, it's wonderful to see you back," Susan began, her tone gentle but probing. "We've been hearing… well, that you've decided against further treatment?"

Ruth offered a calm smile, though a flicker of apprehension crossed her eyes. "That's right. I've chosen to leave my healing in *Gott's* hands."

Esther leaned forward; her brow furrowed. "But what if… what if it's not enough? The doctors are there for a reason, to guide us in these things."

Susan nodded in agreement. "We just don't want to see you take any unnecessary risks. This decision… it's such a big one."

Emma, who had been busy arranging cookies on a tray, stepped in quickly. "Ladies, she has thought long and hard about this. Her faith is stronger than ever, and I've seen how at peace she's been. We need to trust that *Gott* is guiding her."

Though the women nodded, their uneasy glances lingered. Ruth could feel the weight of their doubt settling over her like a cloud. She pressed her hands against the counter, grounding herself.

"I appreciate your love and concern," Ruth said, "but I've come to realize that shielding myself from negative talk is just as important as shielding my body from harm. Doubts and fear can be just as damaging as any illness."

Her friends exchanged glances, their expressions softening,

but Susan spoke again. "We mean no harm. It's just that sometimes fear is a natural part of caring for someone we love."

Emma placed a hand on Ruth's shoulder. "And fear is exactly what we need to give over to the Lord. My *mamm's* decision isn't one she's made lightly. She's trusting *Gott* in all circumstances."

Ruth nodded, her smile returning, but inside, doubt clawed at the edges of her peace. As the conversation shifted to lighter topics, her mind wandered, replaying her friends' words.

Later, when the bakery emptied out, Ruth found herself alone for a moment, leaning against the counter. She closed her eyes, whispering a prayer. *"Lord, strengthen my heart. Remind me of Your promises. I chose to trust You, and I will not let fear cloud my path."*

The door creaked open, and Emma returned from the kitchen with a fresh tray of pastries. "You alright, *Mamm*?"

Ruth opened her eyes. "*Jah*, I am now."

***

Ruth eased into bed beside Levi, her head finding its familiar place on his shoulder. The rhythm of his steady breathing usually brought her comfort, but tonight, her thoughts churned like a restless wind. They lay in the stillness for a while.

After a few moments, Levi asked, "What's troubling you?"

Ruth shifted slightly, her fingers landing on Levi's chest. "The women at the bakery," she started hesitantly. "They… they don't understand why I've chosen not to take the prevention drug. They think I'm being reckless, not doing everything the doctors suggested."

Levi stayed silent, his hand covering hers, urging her to continue.

"They meant well," she added quickly. "But their words have been echoing in my head all day. And now…" Her voice cracked as she whispered, "Levi, tell me I'm not wrong. Please tell me you're okay with my decision."

Levi turned a tad, looking into her eyes. "When have you ever made a decision without seeking *Gott's* guidance? You've prayed about this, and you've found peace in your choice. That peace is *Gott's* assurance, not something to be dismissed."

She looked down, her voice hardly audible. "But what if it's not enough? What if they're right?"

Levi cupped her hand in his. "Fear has a way of creeping in, making us question even the clearest paths. But you've done more than most would. You've changed your diet, you're active, and I can see the difference in you. You're healthier now than before your surgery."

He paused, letting his words sink in before continuing. "You've put your trust in *Gott*, and that's more powerful than any medicine."

Ruth's eyes shimmered with tears, and she leaned into Levi, drawing strength from his unwavering support. "Thank you," she whispered. "Sometimes, I just need to hear it out loud."

Levi pressed a kiss to her temple. "Keep your heart focused on where your peace comes from."

The room fell silent again, but this time, the quiet was filled with a renewed sense of calm. Ruth closed her eyes, the tension from earlier melting away as she felt anchored by Levi's faith and their shared trust in *Gott's* plan.

***

It was a quiet August morning, and the scent of freshly mowed grass seeped through the open kitchen window. Ruth carried a glass of iced tea in one hand as she made her way to the dresser in her bedroom. She intended to reorganize a few drawers, but her hand paused when she touched something familiar: a leather-bound journal, edges softened by time.

She pulled it out and gently ran her fingers over the cover of Stella's journal. Memories flooded back of her dear friend's strength and unwavering faith during her own battle. Ruth had tucked it away after Stella's passing, unable to open it until now.

She took the journal to the front porch, settling onto the swing. The air was warm and heavy with a summer scent as Ruth opened the journal and began reading.

One entry caught her eye, written in Stella's steady hand:

"The doctors say my time is short, but they don't decide my fate. I choose to trust in His plan, no matter how painful the journey. Even when I'm afraid, I know He walks beside me."

Ruth's eyes filled with tears. She turned the page to find another entry:

"When fear tries to consume me, I remind myself that my strength doesn't come from within—it comes from Him. The world offers no guarantees, but my hope isn't in the world. It's in the One who never changes."

Ruth sighed deeply, her heart both heavy and comforted. Stella had been a pillar of faith, even in her darkest hours. Ruth thought of Wilma, who was now fighting her own battle. She saw parallels between Stella's journey and Wilma's, and a sense of purpose stirred within her.

She picked up the journal, adding a handwritten note to the cover.

Dear Wilma,

This journal belonged to my dear friend Stella, who walked a similar path to yours. I pray her words will offer you comfort in the coming months.

Ruth

Setting the journal aside, Ruth returned to the kitchen for another glass of tea. She paused on her way back to the swing, enjoying the sun-drenched yard's peaceful sight. Birds flitted between trees, and the soft rustle of the turning leaves in the gentle breeze reminded her of *Gott's* ever-present peace.

CHAPTER 15

The kitchen was quiet except for the soft click of the clock on the wall. Ruth set a small, worn journal on the table in front of Wilma, her fingers lingering for a moment on its faded cover.

"I found this while tidying up," Ruth said. "It belonged to my dear friend Stella. She wrote about her journey during her own battle. I thought… maybe it could bring you some comfort."

Wilma hesitated, then picked up the journal, her fingers brushing over the well-loved pages. She opened it, reading a passage aloud. "'Even in the darkest nights, I remind myself that the stars are always there, even if I can't see them.'" Wilma's voice wavered, her eyes misting. "She sounds like she was incredible."

"She was," Ruth said, her voice warm with memory. "She faced her journey with courage and faith, even when the world around her tried to steal her hope."

Wilma nodded, closing the journal gently. "Thank you. I'll keep this close and read it later."

Ruth set a steaming pot of herbal tea on the table as Wilma cradled Stella's journal in her hands. The sound of footsteps on the porch interrupted the peaceful hum of the late afternoon. Moments later, Emma and Katie entered, their faces bright with curiosity.

"Well, what's this?" Katie asked, her arms laden with fresh vegetables from the garden. "Looks like we came just in time."

Emma followed, instructing the boys to watch their *schwester* in the other room while they visited with *Grossmommi* and Wilma. "We closed the bakery early and figured you'd be up for some company."

Ruth smiled, but before she could reply, Wilma took a deep breath, setting the journal aside. "I'm glad you're all here. There's something I need to share."

The room quieted as the three women turned their attention to her.

"Seth wants to get married next week," Wilma said, her voice wavering. "And I... I don't know how to pull it off. Without a mother or sisters to help, it feels impossible."

Katie's eyes widened. "Next week? *Ach*, that's hardly any time at all!"

Emma grinned. "But you've got us now. We'll make it happen."

Wilma blinked, overwhelmed. "Really?"

"Of course," Ruth said, her tone steady and reassuring. "We'll start with the dress. What do you have in mind?"

Wilma hesitated. "Something simple. I'm not into all the frills and lace."

Ruth nodded, already envisioning a modest yet elegant design. "How about a soft cotton gown, with delicate embroidery at the hem and sleeves? It'll be light and comfortable, perfect for a late summer wedding."

Wilma's eyes lit up. "That sounds lovely."

Emma leaned in. "And the cake? I'll bake it myself. What's your favorite flavor?"

"Lemon with raspberry filling," Wilma replied, her smile growing. "It was my mom's favorite."

Emma jotted down notes. "Done. We'll decorate it with fresh flowers and berries."

Katie clapped her hands. "And for the venue, we'll use the strawberry barn. We can string up fairy lights and drape some fabric to soften the beams. It'll be charming."

Wilma's breath hitched, emotion welling up. "I don't know how to thank you all."

Emma smiled and replied, "You don't need to thank us. We're family now."

The women spent the rest of the afternoon planning, their laughter and ideas filling the kitchen. By the time the sun dipped below the horizon, Wilma felt like a true part of the Yoder family.

Ruth watched the young woman, her heart full. As they finalized the details, she silently thanked *Gott* for placing Wilma in her life. It was clear now more than ever. She was meant to be the mother figure Wilma needed.

***

Wilma closed the car door with a sigh, letting the quiet wrap around her. The warmth of Ruth's home still clung to her thoughts, and her phone buzzed to life. The surgeon's name lit up the screen, and her stomach tightened.

Her thumb hovered before she answered. "This is Wilma."

"Hi, Wilma. It's Dr. Jameston. I wanted to discuss the

results of your latest scans."

Wilma's breath hitched. She gripped the steering wheel as the doctor's words poured through the receiver. The tumors hadn't responded as hoped. Surgery was still an option, but it would be more complex, and immediate action was recommended.

When Wilma failed to respond, he added, "There's still hope. We just need to be more aggressive moving forward."

Wilma thanked him and ended the call, her hands trembling as she placed the phone back in her lap. The weight of the news pressed down on her chest, squeezing out a shaky exhale. She glanced toward Ruth's house, the soft light from the porch a beacon of comfort.

For a fleeting moment, she considered going back. Ruth would know what to say. She always did. But then she imagined her face, the excitement in her eyes when they talked about the wedding. She couldn't take that from her. Not now. And then there was Seth. How could she shatter his dreams again?

Tears blurred her vision as she whispered, "Not today."

She wiped her cheeks, started the engine, and pulled away from Ruth's home, the road ahead a blur of uncertainty. With each passing mile, the weight of her secret bore down on her, but she resolved to carry it alone—for now. After all, she wasn't just fighting for herself; she was fighting for the life she had only just begun to hope for again.

****

The kitchen carried the scent of supper baking, mingling with the faint hum of cicadas from the open window. Ruth worked diligently, her fingers skillfully pinning fabric as Wilma stood on the wooden stool, arms outstretched.

"Hold still now," Ruth murmured, her voice calm but focused. "I want this seam to fall just right."

Wilma glanced down, her lips curving into a soft smile. "I don't think I've ever had anything made just for me before."

Ruth paused. "There's something special about creating with your hands. Each stitch carries care and prayer. It's my way of blessing your new journey."

Touched, Wilma swallowed back the lump in her throat, masking her emotion with a light joke. "Well, I'll need all the help I can get to keep from tripping over my own feet."

Ruth chuckled, stepping back to assess her work. Their conversation drifted as Ruth continued pinning the hem. The weight of Wilma's thoughts surfaced again.

"I've been thinking," Wilma admitted, her voice quieter now. "Seth and I haven't really talked about kids since… you know… everything."

Ruth stilled her hands, looking up with a steady gaze. "Marriage is a covenant, not a transaction. Seth's love for you isn't tied to what you can or can't give him."

Wilma sighed, the corners of her mouth lifting faintly. "You always know how to make things sound so simple."

Ruth tried to smile through the pins she held between her lips.

Later, as the dress fitting neared its end, Wilma couldn't help but shift the topic to something more lighthearted. "So, Ruth, tell me more about these Amish wedding traditions. I need to know what I'm missing out on."

Ruth's cheeks flushed, and she laughed gracefully. "Well, after the wedding, we spend weeks visiting family and friends as a couple. It's a way to introduce ourselves as husband and wife."

Wilma's eyes widened, a playful grin spreading across her face. "You're telling me your honeymoon is basically a traveling meet-and-greet?"

Ruth laughed; her laughter soft but genuine. "It's a time for fellowship, not for the newlywed luxuries you *Englisch* might have."

Wilma shook her head, giggling. "If Seth tried that, I'd tell him he's on solo tour duty."

The two women shared a hearty laugh, their spirits lifting in the warm light of early evening. But even as the laughter echoed lightly through the room, Wilma caught a flicker of something in Ruth's expression—perhaps a shadow of concern that Ruth didn't quite manage to hide. Wilma had seen it before, and it always reminded her of how deeply Ruth cared, not just in words but in every little action.

She leaned back, letting the moment settle. Despite her earlier worries, Wilma realized she felt less weighed down. Ruth's calm and trusting words hadn't fallen on deaf ears. They had taken root, slowly but surely, weaving their way into her often restless heart. There was a peace there now… a peace she couldn't entirely explain.

It wasn't that the worry was gone, it was just different. Whenever a wave of fear threatened to wash over her, she stopped, breathed, and reminded herself to trust in the Lord and nothing else.

"You know," Wilma said quietly, more to herself than Ruth, "I'm still scared. But it doesn't feel like it used to. Like it's going to swallow me whole."

Ruth nodded; her eyes filled with understanding. "That's *Gott's* peace. It's a gift, and it grows stronger the more you lean on Him."

Wilma smiled, her heart lighter. "Maybe. Or maybe it's just you rubbing off on me, always so calm and steady."

Ruth chuckled. "I have my moments, but even I must remind myself daily to trust."

***

The warm glow of the kerosene lamp flickered casually in the corner of Ruth's living room as the women gathered. The hum of laughter and quiet conversations filled the space, wrapping them in a cocoon of companionship on the eve of Wilma's big day. She sat at the center of it all, her cheeks flushed from laughter, surrounded by Ruth, Katie, Emma, and Janel.

Wilma tilted her head back against the cushion and grinned. "So, tomorrow, I'll officially become Mrs. Seth Trenton. How's that for a twist?" She glanced at Janel, raising an eyebrow. "Think Seth can handle me forever?"

Janel smirked. "If he's smart, he'll let you think you're in charge."

Katie giggled, her face already pink from Wilma's teasing earlier. "You don't hold back, do you?"

"Not when I'm with my sisters," Wilma said, her tone light yet sincere. "And make no mistake, you're all the sisters I never had."

"I mean, who knew I'd end up with not one, not two, but *three* sisters?" Wilma teased, gesturing dramatically to Emma, Katie, and Janel. "You all are the sisters I never had, complete with the scolding and blushing at my jokes." She winked at Emma and Katie, who exchanged wide-eyed looks, their cheeks instantly reddening.

Wilma leaned toward Emma, her eyes sparkling with mischief. "So, Emma, tell me… was Samuel as nervous as Seth when he proposed? Did he stammer, or did he just blurt it out?"

Emma gasped, her hands flying to her face. "Wilma!" she squeaked. "We don't talk about such personal matters!"

Katie, unable to suppress a giggle, shook her head. "She has no shame."

"I'll take that as a yes!" Wilma declared triumphantly, throwing her arms in the air like she'd won a prize. The room erupted in laughter, with Janel nearly spilling her tea.

Ruth smiled; her hands busy with a small sewing project she'd picked up to settle her nerves. "Family isn't just who you're born to," she said, echoing the sentiment she'd often leaned on herself. "Families are knit together, sometimes in the most unexpected ways."

Emma nodded, her voice tender. "It's true. I never imagined I'd find such a close friend in an *Englisher*, but here you are."

Wilma's expression softened. "And here I thought I'd always be on my own after Mom passed." Her voice grew quieter. "I won't lie, sometimes I still wish she were here. Especially now."

The room stilled for a moment, the weight of Wilma's words settling over them and Katie said, "She'd be so proud of you."

After a beat, Janel broke the silence with a cheerful tone. "Okay, enough heavy stuff. Let's talk logistics. Katie, how's the barn looking?"

Katie grinned. "We spent the afternoon decorating. It's

simple, but it's beautiful. The smell of fresh hay mixed with the flowers we gathered—it's perfect."

Emma chimed in, "And the cake is chilling as we speak. Lemon with raspberry filling. Wilma, you'll love it."

"I'm counting on it," Wilma said, her mischievous grin returning.

As the evening wore on, they shared stories, giggles, and even a few quiet tears. Wilma leaned back; her smile softer now. "You know, I wasn't sure about any of this. But sitting here with all of you, I feel… ready."

"That's the beauty of the people in our lives who can fill the gaps where we feel most alone," Ruth added.

The conversation shifted, and Ruth's tone softened as she reflected. "You girls," she said, gesturing to Wilma, Emma, Katie, and even Janel, "have so much to look forward to. Watching your children grow into adults, seeing them find their paths. It's one of the greatest blessings. And the journey? It's filled with joys and heartaches, but every moment is precious."

Katie nodded. "Your strength and wisdom have shaped all of us."

As the clock crept closer to eight, Ruth finally stood. "It's late, and we have a big day ahead, and I'm feeling extra tired this evening. Time to rest."

One by one, the women hugged Wilma, whispering words of encouragement before leaving her to her thoughts. Ruth lingered a moment longer, her heart full as she whispered, "I consider you as much a daughter as the one I raised."

For once, Wilma was left without words. Ruth's heartfelt declaration settled deep within her, more powerful than anything she'd ever heard. She thought, if tomorrow never came, the love and acceptance she found in the Yoder family would have made her life feel complete.

***

The kitchen was filled with the comforting aroma of freshly brewed coffee. Levi leaned against the counter, sipping from his favorite mug, while Ruth set out a simple breakfast of toasted bread and preserves. The stillness of the early morning wrapped around them, broken only by the rhythmic ticking of the wall clock.

Levi's voice broke the quiet. "Hard to believe the day's finally here. Seems like Wilma's been counting down every minute for weeks."

Ruth smiled, though faint lines of worry shadowed her eyes. "It's been a whirlwind, *jah*, but a joyful one. She's ready. And so am I… though I'll admit, I'm glad it's today. I'm not sure how much more excitement either of us could handle."

Levi set his mug down with a soft clink. "You've been looking a bit pale yourself. Maybe you've been pushing too hard, hmm? All this busyness can't be good for you."

Ruth waved her hand dismissively but didn't meet his gaze. "*Ach*, don't fuss. It's just the busyness of the past few weeks catching up, that's all."

He studied her closely, his brow furrowing. "Still, you've been tired more than usual. And Wilma looks more drained each time I see her. Are you sure she's well enough for all this?"

Ruth hesitated, then nodded slowly. "I've noticed it too. She's trying so hard to put on a brave front, but there's a weariness in her eyes. It worries me."

Levi's concern deepened. "Do you think she's ready for the surgery? Or even the wedding today?"

Ruth sighed; the weight of her thoughts heavy. "Wilma's stronger than she gives herself credit for. But I'd be lying if I said I wasn't concerned. I'll keep an eye on her today. The last thing I want is for her to push herself too far."

Levi reached for her hand, his grip firm yet comforting. "And who's keeping an eye on you?"

Ruth gave a soft laugh, meeting his gaze. "You, my *lieb*. Don't you worry about me. Weddings bring a different kind of exhaustion… the good kind."

Levi nodded, though his eyes lingered on her face. "I trust my instincts; they're telling me you're both carrying more than you let on."

Ruth leaned against the counter; her mug cradled in her hands. "Today, we'll celebrate. Tomorrow, I'll rest."

The first hints of dawn filtered through the window, as Ruth set her cup down and leaned her head against Levi's shoulder, the quiet strength of their bond engulfing her.

"It'll be a beautiful day," she murmured, her voice filled with quiet conviction.

Levi squeezed her hand lightly. "It will be. And you've made sure Wilma feels like part of a family again."

Ruth nodded, her eyes glistening. "She is part of our family, Levi. *Gott's* hand has been in all this, every step of the way."

The warmth of the kitchen and the promise of the day ahead wrapped around them like a comforting embrace. Yet, beneath the surface, Ruth's heart carried a mix of joy and unease. She would watch Wilma closely today, praying the young woman could hold onto her strength—and that she could too.

248

CHAPTER 16

The hospital room had the sterile, almost metallic smell of disinfectant mixed with the faintest hint of fresh linens. The steady hum of machines punctuated the air, accompanied by the occasional soft footsteps of nurses in the hallway. Wilma lay in the adjustable bed, her hands fiddling with the edge of the hospital blanket, trying to keep the mood light despite the tension hanging in the air.

She glanced over at Seth, who sat beside her, his face etched with worry. "You know," she teased, her voice playful but soft, "this is exactly what you signed up for when you said 'I do' last week. Too late to back out now, Mr. Trenton."

Seth gave a small chuckle, but the weight in his eyes didn't lift. "I wouldn't back out for anything," he said, squeezing her hand. "But if I could trade places with you…"

Wilma waved him off with a grin. "Oh, please. You'd be useless in this bed, all fidgety and complaining about the hospital food. Leave the tough stuff to me."

Seth shook his head, half-smiling. He leaned forward, kissing her forehead softly.

Ruth moved to sit closer to Wilma, her calm presence filling the space.

Wilma's smile faltered, her voice dropping to a whisper. "Ruth… I'm a little nervous."

Ruth squeezed her hand gently. "It's okay to be scared, *lieb*. But you're not alone in this. *Gott* is with you every step of the way, and so are we."

Wilma nodded, her eyes glistening. "I've been thinking a lot about everything you've taught me… about trusting Him, even when it's hard. I don't know what's going to happen, but I feel… different." Wilma swallowed hard; her voice thick with emotion. "Ruth, I don't know how to thank you. You've been like a mother to me, guiding me through all this. No matter what happens next, I'll always be grateful for your friendship."

The two women sat in silence for a moment, the weight of unspoken emotions hanging between them. "You're stronger than you think. And no matter what, you have a family now— one that will always be here for you."

The soft knock on the door signaled the nurse's arrival. "It's time, Mrs. Trenton," she said gently.

Wilma glanced at Ruth and Seth, a small smile tugging at the corners of her mouth. "Well, here goes nothing."

Seth stood abruptly as the nurse began preparing to wheel Wilma out. He moved to the bedside, taking her hand in both of his. "Wait," he said, his voice quiet but firm. "Just a minute."

He leaned down, his forehead lightly touching hers, and spoke softly. "My love, you're the bravest person I know. And when this is over, we're going to live the life we dreamed of, no matter what it looks like."

Wilma's eyes filled with tears, but she forced a smile. "I hope you're ready to wait on me hand and foot for the next few weeks."

Seth laughed, his thumb brushing away a tear from her cheek. "As long as we're together, I'll do anything you want."

Ruth stood quietly by, her heart swelling at the tender exchange. As they wheeled Wilma toward the operating room, Ruth and Seth exchanged a solemn glance of shared hope and quiet strength.

Before disappearing down the hallway, Wilma turned her head toward them, her voice faint but playful. "Don't forget—no flowers unless they come with pizza."

Seth chuckled, his love for her shining through the worry in his eyes. "Noted, Mrs. Trenton. Noted."

***

The early morning light streamed through Wilma's apartment window as Seth tenderly adjusted the pillows behind her back. She winced vaguely, and he paused, concern etched into his face.

"Too much?" he asked, his voice tender.

Wilma shook her head with a small smile. "No, just enough. I'm fine, Seth, really."

But they both knew better. Each movement was a reminder of her surgery, of the battle her body was waging to heal. Seth hovered close, his protective nature on full display, ready to help with even the smallest tasks.

Ruth arrived not long after, balancing a tray filled with a hearty homemade meal. The comforting aroma of her chicken noodle soup filled the room as she set it down on the kitchen counter. "Thought you might need this," Ruth said, smiling warmly as she peeked into the living room.

Wilma glanced up, her face a mixture of gratitude and

weariness. "Ruth, you're going to spoil us."

"*Ach*, nonsense," Ruth said, waving a hand dismissively. "If you're going to get your strength back, you'll need good food in your belly."

Ruth pulled a new small leather-bound journal from her bag. "I brought something for you," she said, handing it over.

"What's this?" Wilma asked, running her fingers over the worn cover.

"It's a journal. Something to help you sort through your thoughts," Ruth explained.

Wilma hesitated. "I'm not much of a writer."

"You don't have to be," Ruth said. "Sometimes, putting your thoughts on paper can bring a clarity you didn't know you needed."

Wilma nodded slowly, her grip on the journal tightening. "Maybe I'll give it a try."

Later that afternoon, Wilma tried to distract herself by flipping through a magazine, but her mind kept wandering. She caught her reflection in the mirror across the room and hastily looked away. The unfamiliar image of herself... bandaged and fragile... was difficult to reconcile with the person she used to be.

"I feel like a stranger in my own skin," she admitted in a whisper more to herself than anyone else.

Seth, sitting nearby, looked up from his book. "You're still you," he said gently but firmly. "Nothing about that has changed."

Her eyes filled with tears she didn't want to shed. "It's hard to believe that when I don't even recognize myself."

Seth moved to sit beside her, reassuringly touching her without saying a word.

As they grew quiet again, Wilma opened her new journal and stared at the blank page. She hesitated, then began to write:

Today was hard. But I'm learning to lean on others more than I ever have before. Maybe that's the lesson in all this— learning to let go, to trust, to have faith in what I can't control.

She set the pen down and let out a long breath. Ruth's words played in her mind, offering a small but significant sense of peace.

***

The oil lamp above the table danced shadows around the

Yoder kitchen as Ruth stood at the sink, washing the last supper dishes. The soft clink of plates and the steady rhythm of water splashing against the porcelain filled the room. She paused briefly, resting her hands on the edge of the sink, and took a deep breath, willing away the persistent heaviness in her chest.

Levi entered, carrying his coffee mug, placed it on the counter, and eyed Ruth with concern and caution. "You've been working too hard today. Why don't you let me finish up?"

Ruth waved him off with a gentle smile. "*Ach*, I'm fine. It's just a bit of tiredness. Nothing that a good night's sleep won't fix."

Levi frowned but didn't push further. Instead, he quickly picked up a dish towel and dried the plates. Katie stepped in through the back door, carrying little Daniel Jr.on her hip. She took one look at her *mamm* and exchanged a worried glance with her *datt*.

"*Mamm*, you've been looking pale these past few days," Katie said sensitively. "Are you sure you're feeling okay?"

Ruth turned from the sink, wiping her hands on her apron. "I appreciate your concern, but I'm feeling well enough. The cooler weather's just making me a bit sluggish, that's all." She reached out and delicately stroked Daniel Jr.'s cheek, her smile warming her face.

***

Later that night, as the house settled into its quiet routine, Ruth sat at her writing desk. The small journal Stella had once given her lay open, and she picked up her pen, hesitating only briefly before writing:

Today, I felt the weight of my body's limits, a subtle reminder that I am but a vessel in Gott's hands. Whatever He wills, I will walk that path with faith, knowing He's already gone before me.

She paused, tapping the pen against the page, and then added:

Even in weariness, I am reminded of His strength. My life has been full of His mercy, and I can only pray I've fulfilled His purpose as His servant on this earth.

Ruth closed the journal and sat back, gazing out the window at the stars peeking through the autumn sky. Despite the weariness in her bones, a deep peace settled over her heart. She whispered a quiet prayer, thanking *Gott* for His guidance and asking for continued strength, whatever the days ahead might bring.

***

Six weeks later, the sun poured through the oncology center's tall glass windows, bathing the lobby in light. Wilma sat with her hands folded in her lap, gazing outside at the bustling world beyond. Her hair was still short, just beginning to grow back, but her spirit was undeniably stronger even though her chemo was about to start again. Seth sat beside her, his comforting presence a steady anchor.

A soft sniffle broke her thoughts. Wilma turned to see an older woman seated beside her, clutching a tissue and nervously twisting it in her hands. Her eyes were red-rimmed, and her foot tapped anxiously against the polished floor.

"You here for the first time?" Wilma asked, her voice low and soothing.

The woman nodded; her lips pressed tightly together. "I just… I don't know how I'm going to do this," she whispered, her voice trembling. "It's all so overwhelming."

Wilma smiled, a soft and knowing expression. "I get it. The first time I sat in this very spot, I felt like my whole world was spinning out of control, but someone told me something that helped." She leaned in a little, her tone warm. "It's okay to feel scared. But you don't have to walk this road alone. There's strength in leaning on others, and even more in trusting that you'll find peace as you go."

The woman blinked, her expression softening. "Did it… did it get easier?"

"Not always," Wilma admitted. "But I learned to take it one day at a time. And each day, I found little pieces of hope, even in the hardest moments." She reached over and lightly touched the woman's hand. "You'll find your strength too."

The older woman nodded, a faint smile forming through her tears. "Thank you. I needed to hear that."

Seth, who had been listening quietly, reached over and gave Wilma's hand a gentle squeeze. They exchanged a glance, a silent acknowledgment of how far she had come. Wilma had once been in that very seat, terrified and unsure, and now she was offering the same comfort and wisdom Ruth had once given her.

As the older woman rose when her name was called, she gave Wilma a grateful nod. Wilma leaned back in her chair; her heart full.

Seth leaned in and whispered, "You've become someone's Ruth."

Wilma chuckled softly, glancing at him. "Well, I had a pretty great teacher."

Wilma sat with her fingers laced through Seth's as they waited for her name to be called. She glanced at Seth, who was scrolling through his phone. "You've gotten quiet over there. Are you Googling how to keep a stubborn wife from cracking bad jokes in a serious situation?"

Seth smirked. "No, but I should be. Don't think for a second I'm letting you try out new material on the nurses."

Before Wilma could retort, a nurse with a kind smile appeared in the doorway. "Wilma Trenton?"

"That's me," Wilma said, standing and tugging Seth up with her. "Don't leave me unsupervised; I might charm the nurses too much."

The nurse chuckled. "I'll keep an eye on her," she told Seth. "But you're welcome to join us."

The treatment room was softly lit and lined with recliners, each equipped with a small table and a blanket. Wilma remembered the nerves she'd felt the first time she walked into a similar room, but today, there was a calmness she couldn't quite explain. It wasn't just the warmth of Seth's hand in hers… it was something deeper, a quiet assurance that had grown over time.

As she settled into the chair, the nurse introduced herself as Pam. "First round post-surgery, right? How are you feeling?"

"Honestly? A lot better than the first time I did this," Wilma said. "That time, I was convinced the whole building was going to collapse on me. Now, I'm just hoping the snacks are good."

Pam laughed as she began setting up the IV line. "You're in luck, we have ginger ale and crackers. Five-star dining right here."

"Perfect," Wilma replied. "And Seth brought reinforcements." She nodded toward the small bag he was holding.

"I came prepared," Seth said, pulling out a thermos and a container of homemade trail mix. "Her standards are high."

Pam glanced at Wilma with a knowing smile. "You've got a good one there."

"Oh, I know," Wilma said, squeezing Seth's hand. "He just won't admit I trained him well."

As Pam continued her work, she said, "I have to say, you seem remarkably calm. Most people are nervous at this stage."

Wilma tilted her head thoughtfully. "I was last time. Terrified, actually. But I had a dear friend who reminded me that trust in something bigger than myself is what matters most. She taught me how to lean on faith, even when everything feels uncertain."

Pam nodded as she adjusted the IV. "I see a lot of patients come through here. Some are so weighed down by fear and hopelessness, and others—like you—come in with a sense of calm assurance. It makes a world of difference."

Wilma grinned. "Well, peace helps, but so does a solid sense of humor. I mean, if I can't make someone laugh in this chair, what's the point?"

Pam laughed. "That's a good attitude to have."

As Pam finished setting up, Seth pulled his chair closer and held Wilma's hand again. "Are you sure you're okay?" he asked quietly.

"I'm okay," Wilma said, her voice steady. "I really am. And if I'm not, I've got you to remind me."

As the infusion began, Wilma leaned back in the chair, letting the warmth of Seth's presence and Pam's kindness settle over her. The sun outside the windows felt brighter than it had in months, and for the first time in a long time, Wilma felt like the future was something to look forward to rather than fear.

CHAPTER 17

Ruth stepped onto the front porch, her woolen shawl draped over her shoulders as she settled into the old wooden rocker. The air carried the crisp bite of fall, mingled with the earthy aroma of fallen leaves and the faint scent of wood smoke from a nearby farm. The horizon glowed with hues of orange and gold, a testament to the changing season, while the trees around the Yoder farm stood proudly adorned in their last few leaves.

She placed her journal and two cream-colored envelopes on the small table beside her. With a deep breath, she picked up her pen and began to write.

This year has been one of trials and triumphs, Lord. You've shown me your hand in ways I never imagined. From my own battle with illness to guiding Wilma through hers, you've made your purpose clear. Thank you for allowing me to be your hands and feet during this season. I pray I've served you well, showing your light to those who needed it most.

Wilma, especially, has been such a blessing. She came into my life at just the right time, reminding me that your plans are far greater than my own. Her courage has inspired me, and I pray that I've offered her the strength and guidance she needed to see your faithfulness through the storm. Thank you for this path, even when it was hard to see the end.

Ruth closed the journal and picked up the first envelope, which was addressed to Katie. She hesitated for a moment, gathering her thoughts, then began to write. The words came easily, flowing from a heart full of love and wisdom, as she recounted memories, offered encouragement, and shared her hopes for Katie's future.

After sealing Katie's letter, she turned to the second envelope addressed to Wilma. A faint smile played on her lips as she considered the young woman who had so promptly become like a daughter to her. The weight of this year's journey pressed on her as she wrote, filling the page with words she prayed would comfort and guide Wilma long after the ink had dried.

As the sun dipped lower, highlighting the farm, Ruth leaned back in the rocker, listening to the soft rustle of leaves. She whispered a quiet prayer, her voice barely audible in the stillness of the evening.

"Lord, let these letters carry your wisdom and love. May they be a source of comfort and strength in the days to come."

She set the letters aside, her heart full yet at peace. The sound of her grandchildren laughing in the distance brought a contented smile to her face. The giggles drifted toward her, growing louder with each passing second. Her heart swelled as she watched Otto and Owen race ahead, their identical faces lit with joy, while Ella and Mary trailed behind, arms linked in a playful dance.

"Grossmommi! Grossmommi!" Otto called; his cheeks flushed from running. "We made the biggest pile of leaves ever! Come see!"

Ruth laughed, setting aside her cup. "*Ach*, Otto, you'll have to show me later. Come up here first so I can get a proper hug!"

The boys bounded up the porch steps, followed by Ella and Mary, who each took one of Ruth's hands, their small fingers squeezing tightly. Owen leaned in for a hug, his grin mischievous. "We're making you a leaf throne, *Grossmommi!*"

"A leaf throne? For me?" Ruth exclaimed, her eyes sparkling. "I suppose that means I'm a queen today."

"You're always the queen!" Ella chimed in, her braids bouncing as she climbed onto Ruth's lap. Ruth kissed the top of her granddaughter's head, her hair smelling faintly of lavender soap.

Mary, the quieter of the two girls, tugged Ruth's sleeve. "*Grossmommi*, can we bake cookies later? *Datt* said you might like that."

"Cookies?" Ruth tilted her head in mock thoughtfulness.

The twins, growing restless, tugged Ruth's apron. "Come on, *Grossmommi*! Let's show you the leaf pile!"

Ruth pushed herself up from the rocking chair with a playful groan, Ella and Mary holding onto her skirt as the boys raced back toward the yard. She paused at the top of the steps, her heart filled with a quiet joy as she watched them dart between the trees, their laughter echoing against the golden hues of falling leaves.

"Hurry!" Owen called, waving an arm. "Your throne's ready!"

"Well, I suppose I can't keep my royal subjects waiting," Ruth said, a grin spreading across her face.

The girls giggled as they followed her down the steps and across the yard. The boys had indeed built a makeshift "throne" of leaves, and Ruth indulged them by sitting on it as they crowned her with a garland of twigs and colorful leaves.

Ruth laughed with her grandchildren, savoring the moment. She felt the warmth of the sun on her face and the love of her family all around her. As the children scampered off to gather more leaves, Ruth stood and gazed at them, her heart swelling with gratitude.

In her heart, Ruth whispered a prayer: *Thank You, Lord, for this moment. For these precious little ones, for this love that fills my days, and for the laughter that makes my soul light.*

The scene stayed with her as they all walked back to the porch together, Ruth holding Mary's and Ella's hands while Otto and Owen ran ahead. She knew that this memory, like so many others, would stay etched in her heart forever.

***

The next morning, the warm, yeasty aroma of rising bread filled the kitchen as Ruth kneaded the dough on the countertop. The rhythmic motion soothed her, grounding her in the familiar tasks of homemaking. She glanced at the old black stove, its polished surface glinting in the morning light. Her eyes lingered on the smooth, cast-iron edge, and a tender smile crossed her face.

She remembered the day it arrived, nearly forty years ago. She and Levi had just moved into the big *haus*, newly married and brimming with hope, though their pockets were light. The stove had been a gift—a quiet surprise—and with it came a letter from her *mamm*. Ruth could still hear her mother's voice in the words she wrote, a bittersweet mixture of love and farewell.

"Dear Daughter," her mother had written, *"if you're reading this, then Gott has finally called me home…"* Ruth's chest tightened as she recalled the lines about love, legacy, and family… the reminder that a woman's stove is the heart of her home.

Ruth could almost feel her mother's hand guiding her as she shaped the loaves of bread, her legacy alive in every action. Her mother's letter had spoken of a life well-lived, of service to *Gott* and family, and of leaving behind a foundation of love and faith.

The letter's final lines always stayed with her: *"Life happens around a stove. Families grow around a stove. A mother's love happens around a stove."* Ruth smiled softly, her heart warmed by the memory.

After placing the dough on the counter to rise, Ruth rested for a few minutes before moving on to her next task. The rhythmic hum of the broom against the kitchen floor mingled with the faint crackle of the wood stove. Ruth wiped her brow, feeling the weariness settle in her bones. The morning had been a whirlwind of baking, tidying, and setting things out for the quilting bee.

She glanced at the half-finished quilt stretched over the frame in the corner, its wedding ring pattern coming together with each stitch. It was meant for Wilma, a labor of love and a tangible reminder of their bond.

With the house ready and the aroma of freshly baked bread lingering in the air, Ruth poured herself a cup of tea. She carried it out to the front porch, craving a moment of stillness before her friends arrived.

The air was crisp, the kind that hinted at the season's impending change. Snowflakes danced informally on the breeze, melting as they kissed the earth. Ruth pulled her sweater tighter around her shoulders, letting the steam from her tea rise and warm her face. She leaned back on the porch swing, the creak of the wood a familiar comfort.

Her gaze wandered over the last of the leaves clung

stubbornly to the branches, a gentle reminder of winter's approach. She closed her eyes for a moment, soaking in the crispness of morning.

She whispered a quiet prayer, her breath mingling with the steam. *"Thank you, Lord, for your guidance and strength. May this quilt wrap Wilma in your love and remind her that she is never alone."*

The sound of horses' hooves on gravel pulled Ruth from her thoughts. Susan's buggy came into view, the horses' breath visible in the chilly air. She stood, brushing a stray lock of hair from her face, and greeted her friend with a warm smile.

As she made her way to the porch, Ruth felt a renewed sense of purpose. Today wasn't just about finishing the quilt; it was about fellowship, laughter, and the shared work of women coming together; a tradition as old as the stitches they were about to sew.

***

The quilt frame sat like a centerpiece, its fabric stretched taut and ready for the final stitches. Emma, Katie, Susan, and Ruth sat around it, their needles moving in and out with practiced precision. The rhythmic motion of stitching was a comfort, the sound of thread pulling through fabric punctuating their gentle conversation.

Emma's gaze lingered on Ruth, her brow furrowing. "*Mamm*, let me take over your section."

Ruth waved her off with a teasing smile. "*Ach, denki*. My arm is cramping up. I'll just sit here and supervise for a few minutes. I'll make sure you're not skipping any stitches."

Katie chuckled. "*Mamm*, I think we've got it. You've taught us well."

Ruth leaned back in her chair, letting the warmth of the room and the sound of their voices wash over her. "It's my motherly duty to pass down all the secrets of being a good and useful Amish woman. Not that you need much help, but it's good to keep you on your toes."

The women laughed, and even Emma couldn't suppress a grin. "Just don't critique too hard, *Mamm*, or I'll hand the needle back lickety-split."

Ruth's eyes softened as she watched her daughters. She felt a deep sense of gratitude for moments like this, for the ability to share in the joys and trials of their lives. Her heart swelled with pride, knowing that the skills and values she had instilled in them would carry on.

Emma spoke up, her tone thoughtful. "It's a blessing, really, to have these moments. Life gets so busy, but this—this is what it's all about."

Ruth nodded, her voice quiet. "*Jah*, it is. Every stitch we make, every moment we share, all adds up to something bigger than ourselves."

The women worked in silence for a while, the room filled with the peaceful hum of their labor. Outside, the sky deepened as the day slowly giving way to night. The quilt, nearly finished, was a testament to their love and dedication to their new *Englisch* friend.

***

Later that evening, Ruth moved slowly through the quiet house, her hands steadying the back of each chair as she tidied up from the quilting bee. The hum of conversation and laughter still echoed faintly in her ears, but now the house was wrapped in silence. She reached for a quilt folded neatly on the sofa, waiting for her to bind it off, but the sudden wave of lightheadedness stopped her mid-motion. Gripping the table's edge, she steadied herself, breathing deeply to stave off the fainting spell.

"Ruth?" Levi's voice was calm but concerned as he stepped into the room. He crossed the space quickly, his calloused hands gently grasping her arms. "You're pushing yourself too hard. Come, lie down."

Ruth allowed herself to be guided, and the warmth of Levi's hand on the small of her back comforted her. He led her to their bedroom, helping her settle under the familiar weight of their handmade quilt. She smiled tiredly as he pulled the chair closer to her bedside and sat down.

"I'm fine, Levi. Just a little dizzy from all the excitement," she reassured him, though her voice lacked its usual conviction. Levi leaned forward, resting his hand on hers. "You've been saying that too often, Ruth. You've done enough, more than enough. It's time to take it easy."

Ruth looked at him, brushing her fingers lightly over his weathered face. "I don't say it enough, but I see how you've carried me these past months. I couldn't have walked this path without you."

Levi's eyes softened, and he squeezed her hand. "You've carried us all, Ruth. You always have. I just do what I can to keep you steady."

A quiet tear slipped down Ruth's cheek. "Levi," she began, her voice faltering for a moment, "I can't imagine a life without you by my side. You've been my greatest blessing, and I thank *Gott* every day for you."

Levi leaned closer, brushing a kiss across her forehead. "And I thank Him for you, every moment."

Ruth closed her eyes, letting the warmth of Levi's presence and the weight of his words comfort her. Though she didn't voice it, her heart whispered a prayer of gratitude for the life they'd built together, knowing deep within that every moment with him was a gift.

As Levi sat beside her, their fingers intertwined, the quiet of their home was the backdrop for her unspoken prayer: *Thank You, Lord, for this perfect love and for the strength You've given us through every season.*

***

The dawn light seeped through the window above the kitchen sink as Ruth hummed softly, reaching for a glass from the cupboard. Her hand trembled slightly, but she steadied it with a deep breath. As she filled the glass with water, the faint tremor betrayed her strength. The glass slipped from her grasp, shattering against the tile floor in a cascade of sharp shards.

Levi hurried in, his face etched with concern. "Are you all right?"

She nodded weakly and eased into a chair at the kitchen table. "I'm fine, Levi," she said, though her pale complexion and the weariness in her voice told another story.

Levi knelt beside her, his hands carefully picking up the glass. "I think it's time you saw the doctor."

Ruth hesitated, the weight of his words settling over her like a heavy blanket. "I'll make an appointment," she whispered, her resolve faltering under his worried gaze.

After breakfast, Levi kissed her forehead before heading out to the barn. Alone, Ruth looked around the quiet kitchen. She gathered herself and forced her way through her morning routine, determined to push back against her body's increasing fragility. She filled a basket with laundry and carried it to the washing room, her steps slow and deliberate. Each movement seemed to draw from a reservoir of strength she wasn't sure she still had.

Once the laundry was started, Ruth climbed the stairs to the bedroom, intending to gather more clothes. The bed looked inviting, a haven of rest she couldn't resist. She set the basket down and stretched out on the quilt, closing her eyes for what she told herself would be just a few minutes.

Her thoughts drifted, carried by the memories of a life richly lived. She saw Levi, younger and strong, laughing as he hoisted Samuel onto his shoulders in the barn. She saw Katie's bright smile as she learned to knead dough for the first time. The laughter of her grandchildren echoed softly, their tiny hands reaching for her as they played beneath the shade of the old maple tree in the front yard.

Finally, her thoughts turned to Wilma. She whispered a silent prayer, *"Lord, guide her path. Let her feel the strength You've given me, and may she find joy in You."*

Tears slipped unobtrusively down her cheeks as she whispered her silent prayers: A goodbye to each of her children and a blessing for her grandchildren.

Soon, she would see all those that went before her. She wondered what it would be like. She opened her eyes and looked around the darkened room one last time before hearing her name being whispered in the shadows.

Ruth's breathing slowed as the dream world embraced her

fully, the weight of her earthly struggles giving way to a serene joy and the promise of eternal rest.

"Thank You, Lord," she whispered, her voice barely audible. "I'm ready."

A warmth, unlike anything she had ever known, enveloped her like a gentle embrace. The weight of her earthly body faded, and she felt herself being carried—not away from her family but toward something greater. A light brighter than the sun but as soft as a candle's glow surrounded her. It wasn't unfamiliar. It was home.

Her heart swelled with emotion as a melody rose within her—one she had sung a thousand times but now came from a place beyond herself. Tears spilled freely as her voice joined a heavenly chorus that echoed around her, a symphony of peace and praise. *"Holy, holy, holy."*

Tracy Fredrychowski

EPILOGUE

Two years later.

Moonlight sent a soft shadow dancing across Wilma's bedroom walls as she drifted between sleep and wakefulness. In her half-dream state, she found herself standing in a field of flowers. The air was warm, and the sun was low in the sky, adding a calming glow to everything it touched. In the distance, Ruth stood with her hands clasped in front of her, a peaceful smile on her face.

"Ruth?" Wilma whispered, taking a hesitant step forward.

Ruth nodded, her expression serene. "You're doing beautifully," she said, her voice as soft as the tall grass around them. "Motherhood isn't about perfection; it's about presence. Be there for her in the small moments; the ones that seem insignificant. That's where the greatest love grows."

Wilma's throat tightened. "But what if I don't know what to do? What if I make mistakes?"

Ruth smiled wider, her eyes full of gentle wisdom. "You will make mistakes. But love, true love, covers them all. Trust yourself and trust Him."

The distant sound of a baby crying began to weave itself into the dream, pulling Wilma gently toward wakefulness. Ruth's image grew hazy, but her voice lingered. "Remember, she doesn't need a perfect mother. She just needs you."

Wilma's eyes fluttered open, the dream fading but leaving behind a profound sense of peace. Her baby's soft cries came from the bassinet across the room. Wilma sat up, the words from her dream echoing in her heart as she made her way to her daughter.

"Shh, little one," she whispered, gathering her into her arms. "Mama's here."

As she carried the child to the other room to make a bottle, the peace from the dream remained, and there was a steady warmth in her heart. Suddenly, the nervousness she'd been experiencing since bringing baby Ruth home two days earlier faded to be replaced with Ruth's guiding presence.

As Wilma settled into the creaky rocking chair, baby Ruth nestled snugly in her arms, she allowed herself a moment of quiet reflection. The rhythm of the chair, paired with the soft coos of the baby, brought a wave of calm that wrapped around her like a familiar quilt. She glanced toward the bedroom where Seth lay sleeping, his chest rising and falling steadily. His presence, solid and reassuring, had been her anchor through so many storms.

She smiled, remembering the sheer disbelief and joy on his face when they discovered she was pregnant. It had been a miracle, defying all the odds stacked against them after her grueling treatments and hospital stays. That same sense of awe filled her now, holding this tiny life in her arms—a life she once thought she'd never experience.

"Just like Ruth," Wilma whispered, her voice just audible over the gentle rustling of the curtains. "A miracle."

Ruth had entered her life during a season of despair, offering wisdom, love, and an unwavering faith that seemed almost otherworldly. Losing her had left a void so deep that Wilma feared she'd never climb out of it. Yet here she was, feeling an overwhelming joy that rivaled the depth of that grief.

She stroked baby Ruth's soft cheek, marveling at the tiny fingers wrapped around her own. "You're named after someone who showed me the way when I couldn't find it myself," she said, her eyes misting. "She taught me that life is full of seasons.

Some break you, and some rebuild you."

The weight of grief and joy intertwined, but in this moment, the balance tipped toward joy. Baby Ruth stirred, her tiny face scrunching before she relaxed again. Wilma leaned forward, her forehead resting tenderly against her daughter's.

"God's hand was in it all," she murmured. "Even when I couldn't see it, He worked miracles."

The baby let out a soft sigh, and Wilma chuckled quietly, savoring the completeness of this moment. As the first light of dawn crept into the room, she rocked her daughter, her heart full of gratitude for the miracle she now held close.

With baby Ruth snuggled against her mother's shoulder, Wilma opened the small wooden box on the stand next to the chair. She pulled Ruth's letter out, carefully unfolding its crisp pages, and re-read Ruth's tender words.

Dear Wilma,

When I first met you, I saw a spark, a strength you hadn't yet discovered in yourself. You were fighting so many battles, and yet, you didn't give up. You reminded me of myself, and maybe that's why God put us on the same path. He knew we needed each other.

I want you to remember this: Faith isn't about never being afraid; it's about trusting even when you are. It's about knowing that God is in control, even when everything feels out of place. Lean into Him, especially in those moments when you feel weakest. He's there, holding you up, even when you don't feel it.

You've been a blessing to me, more than I could ever put into words. You gave me a purpose in my final season, and you reminded me of the beauty in life's simplest moments.

The journey won't always be easy, but it will always be worth it. Take each day as it comes and never forget that you're surrounded by love—mine, Seth's, and most importantly, God's.

With all my love,

Ruth

Wilma carefully folded the letter, her eyes filled with tears, a mix of sorrow and joy. The words were a balm to her soul, a reminder that even in Ruth's absence, her guidance and love would remain a constant presence in her life forever.

***

Read more from

The Amish Women of Lawrence County Series in

<u>Katie's Amish Journey of Hope</u>

Grief has consumed Katie Miller's life, stealing her joy and leaving her adrift. When the loss of her mother shakes the foundation of her faith, Katie struggles to be the wife and mother her family needs. Her husband, Daniel, watches helplessly as she retreats further into sorrow, while her father, Levi, is lost in his own grief.

Just as Katie feels like she's slipping away, small reminders of her mother's unwavering faith begin to appear. Could these quiet messages from heaven be leading her back to hope? *Katie's Amish Journey of Hope* is a moving story of love, loss, and the power of God's grace to heal even the deepest wounds.

Katie's

Amish Journey of Hope

THE AMISH WOMEN OF LAWRENCE COUNTY SERIES - BOOK 8

Tracy Fredrychowski

PROLOGUE

The noise on the other side of the door only made my anxiety worse as I pressed my back against it. Ella's little fists tapped frivolously, followed by her sweet voice. "*Mamm*, are you coming out? We're hungry."

Mary's voice chimed in, more impatient. "You said we could have snack time after we finished coloring."

And then came Daniel Jr., his tiny toddler feet thudding against the door as he let out a loud wail. "*Mamm*!"

I clenched my eyes shut, clutching the letter in my hand. The familiar texture of the worn paper was both a comfort and a reminder of how many times I'd read these words, hoping for strength. But the weight of *Mamm's* absence was heavier than the comfort her words could bring.

Put Gott first. Be a loving mother. Honor your husband. Be his helpmate.

Each line felt like a task I wasn't strong enough to complete.

How could I put *Gott* first when I felt so lost? How could I be a loving mother when I could barely get through the day? And as for honoring my husband, it felt like I was failing Daniel more with each passing moment.

Daniel Jr.'s wails grew louder, his tiny fists joining his *schwesters'* knocks. "*Maaaamm!*"

"Shhh, Daniel," Ella whispered. "*Mamm's* coming soon."

"Maybe she's crying again," Mary added in a quieter voice. The guilt twisted in my stomach, sharp and unforgiving. My precious children. They didn't understand why their mother wasn't the same anymore, why I spent so much time locked away in this bathroom, clinging to a tattered letter like it held all the answers.

"I'll be out in a minute," I called, though my voice cracked.

I unfolded the letter, my eyes scanning *Mamm's* familiar handwriting. Even now, her words felt like a lifeline, even if they couldn't pull me out of this dark place.

You were chosen for this life, Katie, to love, to nurture, to build a home filled with joy and faith.

But what if I couldn't do it? What if the pieces of me that *Mamm* believed in were gone, buried under layers of grief?

Daniel's sobs softened into hiccups, but the sound of all

three of them waiting on the other side of the door was enough to force me to my feet. I folded the letter carefully and slipped it into my pocket, close to my heart but hidden from view.

Mamm's words echoed in my ears, adding a fresh round of sobs in the back of my throat as I played over *Mamm's* words.

I know someday I won't be here to walk with you through life's joys and sorrows. That thought is hard for me, as I imagine it will be for you. When that time comes, I want you to remember that it's natural to grieve, my sweet girl. That grief is a reflection of how deeply you love, but it is not meant to consume you. When the pain feels heavy, lean into Gott's strength, just as I have in my hardest moments. He will carry you, even when you feel like you cannot take another step.

I placed my hand on the doorknob and took a deep breath. "Alright, I'm coming. Let's get you all that snack."

My voice sounded steadier than I felt, but maybe that was enough. For now, it had to be.

***

Read more about Katie in the eighth book of

The Amish Women of Lawrence County Series.

Katie's Amish Journey of Hope

Katie Miller's world is falling apart. Her mother's passing has left an ache too deep for words, and the once-strong bond of her family is unraveling under the weight of sorrow.

Katie must choose whether to remain lost in grief or embrace the promise of renewal. *Katie's Amish Journey of Hope* is a heartfelt novel about finding joy again, trusting in God's plan, and discovering that love and faith can carry us through even the darkest seasons.

WHAT DID YOU THINK?

First of all, thank you for purchasing *The Amish Women of Lawrence County – Ruth's Amish Words of Faith.* I hope you will enjoy all the books in this series.

You could have picked any number of books to read, but you chose this book, and for that, I am incredibly grateful. I hope it added value and quality to your everyday life. If so, it would be nice to share this book with your friends and family on social media.

If you enjoyed this book and found some benefit in reading it, I'd like to hear from you and hope that you could take some time to post a review on Amazon. Your feedback and support will help me improve my writing craft for future projects.

If you loved visiting Willow Springs, I invite you to sign up for my private email list, where you'll get to explore more of the characters of this Amish Community.

Sign up at https://dl.bookfunnel.com/v9wmnj7kve and download the novella that starts this series, *The Amish Women of Lawrence County.*

GLOSSARY

Pennsylvania Dutch "Deutsch" Words

Ausbund. Amish songbook.

bruder. Brother.

datt. Father or dad.

denki. Thank You.

doddi. Grandfather.

doddi haus. A small house next to the main house.

g'may. Community.

gut meiya. Good morning.

jah. Yes.

kapp. Covering or prayer cap.

kinner. Children.

mamm. Mother or mom.

grossmommi. Grandmother.

nee. No.

Ordnung. Order or set of rules the Amish follow.

schwester. Sister.

singeon. Singing/youth gathering.

The Amish are a religious group typically referred to as Pennsylvania Dutch, Pennsylvania Germans, or Pennsylvania Deutsch. They are descents of early German immigrants to Pennsylvania, and their beliefs center around living a conservative lifestyle. They arrived between the late 1600s and the early 1800s to escape religious persecutions in Europe. They first settled in Pennsylvania with the promise of religious freedom by William Penn. Most Pennsylvania Dutch still speak a variation of their original German language as well as English.

ABOUT THE AUTHOR

Tracy Fredrychowski's life closely mirrors the gentle, simple stories she crafts in her writing. With a passion for the simpler side of life, Tracy regularly shares tips on her website and blog at tracyfredrychowski.com

In northwestern Pennsylvania, Tracy grew up steeping in the virtues of country living. A pivotal moment in her life was the tragic murder of a young Amish woman in her community.

This event profoundly influenced her, compelling her to dedicate her writing to the peaceful lives of the Amish people. Tracy aims to inspire her readers through her stories to embrace a life centered around faith, family, and community.

For those intrigued by the Amish way of life, Tracy extends an invitation to connect with her on Facebook. On her page and group, she shares captivating Amish photography by her friend Jim Fisher and recipes, short stories, and glimpses into her cherished Amish community nestled deep in the heart of northwestern Pennsylvania's Amish County.

Facebook.com/tracyfredrychowskiauthor/

Facebook.com/groups/tracyfredrychowski/

9 798990 610590